SCARLET PRINCESS

ROBIN D. MAHLE
ELLE MADISON

Cover : Moorbooks

Maps: Elle Madison

Copy Editing: Holmes Edits

To all of the Rowans out there who would have gone down that tunnel for a bottle of booze and bad decisions.

"And I was runnin' far away
Would I run off the world someday?
I was dancing in the rain
I felt alive and I can't complain
But now take me home
Take me home where I belong"
Runaway - Aurora

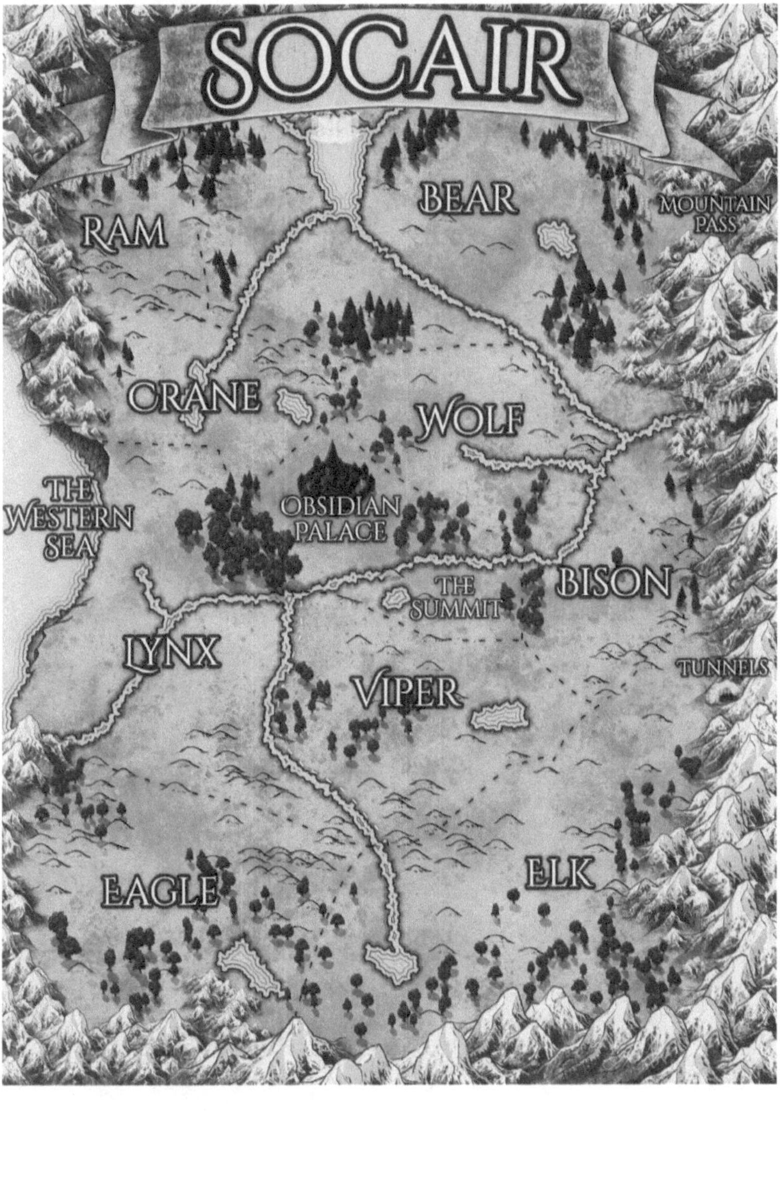
SOCAIR
BEAR
MOUNTAIN PASS
RAM
CRANE
WOLF
THE WESTERN SEA
OBSIDIAN PALACE
BISON
THE SUMMIT
LYNX
TUNNELS
VIPER
EAGLE
ELK

PROLOGUE

Death was a hefty price to pay for vodka.

The last thing I remembered was a thunderous roar echoing down a narrow tunnel. Then, the choice to risk venturing into an enemy kingdom rather than starve to death by the rocks we couldn't move.

Days of wandering down that tunnel, each step leading to more dehydration and eventually, delirium.

Which was probably right about when my cousin Davin and I decided to open a bottle of vodka to keep warm.

Maybe that was where we had gone wrong. We were too incoherent to notice the soldiers creeping in on us, too dizzy to fight back.

Or maybe it was before that, months before that, when I made the decision to go down into the tunnels to begin with.

Either way, it was hard to deny we had erred somewhere along the way when I woke up on the floor of a Socairan dungeon.

CHAPTER 1

My skull was on fire.

Or perhaps there were horses galloping across it, each hoof landing with more force than the last. I blearily opened my eyes, looking around the dimly lit space from the iron bars on three sides of me to a dingy metal chamber pot in the corner.

A dungeon. I was in a dungeon.

Finally, my gaze landed on the blurry outline of my cousin in the cell next to mine. He quirked an eyebrow, though the motion made him wince. He lifted his bound hands to his head as if he could rub it away.

My wrists twitched in sympathy, and I looked down to find the rough fibers of a rope digging into my flesh. Right. They had also tied us up. Bracing my hands on the cold stone floor, I pushed myself into a sitting position, blinking away the stars that edged out my vision.

"Well, if they thought to punish us, the joke is on them. This is a holiday compared to the caves." Davin's voice was rough from disuse.

3

It was true enough. Though it was still freezing, the little air coming in from the tiny cell window was crisp and fresh, nothing like the frigid, stagnant tunnel.

For that matter, the space was open, only bars separating the rows of empty cells.

"Who is *they* exactly?" My mouth felt like it had been glued shut, and my voice came out a quiet rasp.

The Socairans, obviously. But which ones? And where were the other prisoners?

"Stars if I know. The last thing I remember is a cloth coming over my mouth, then nothing until we woke up here." He paused, lifting both hands to push his black locks from where they had fallen into his eyes.

"Which clan do you think we have the pleasure of visiting?" I vaguely registered that I should be panicking, but none of this quite felt real.

Princesses don't get put in dungeons.

Davin made a show of looking around, letting out a low whistle.

"Judging by the superior quality of the chamber pots and the odor wafting from that end of our accommodations," he gestured behind him, "I'd say we were in Clan Dragonbreath."

I snorted out a laugh. "Is that even a real clan?"

"No idea." He shrugged. "But, if it isn't, it should be."

I shook my head, suppressing a shiver.

"We've really done it this time, haven't we?" Davin sighed, scratching at his several days' worth of beard.

"Indeed," I replied, shaking my head in disbelief. "Do you know the last thing Da' said to me? He said, *Damn it,*

4

Rowan! Can I not leave ye fer five minutes without ye running off to do something stupid?"

I did my best imitation of my father's brogue, but the angry tone was eclipsed by an unexpected fit of giggles on that last word. Something stupid, indeed. To think, that had only been referring to him finding me gambling at the village tavern.

What would he think now?

Davin joined me in laughter, and the pounding in my head was well worth putting off the grim thoughts of what our futures might hold.

"Well, the last thing my mother said was, *Try to stay away from the whores this time.*"

At that, I lost it entirely, tears of mirth running down my cheeks. "At least one of us was successful, then," I gasped between breaths. "Unless you were very discreet."

Davin tried to respond, but his guffaws gave way to wheezing. The sound sobered us a little and reminded me how long it had been since we had something other than vodka. I searched around the cell in vain for something to drink.

They had taken our swords and my satchel with the remaining bottles of vodka in it.

Our canteens had run dry at least a day ago, depending on how long we had been in the dungeons. Though, I knew we couldn't have been here for long. My head still swam from the remnants of alcohol in my system mixed with whatever they had drugged us with.

The sound of a throat clearing abruptly cut off my search.

My gaze snapped up to a startlingly handsome face.

Swarthy skin contrasted with pale blonde hair and eyes on the greener side of hazel, eyes that were currently narrowed in a haughty sort of bafflement, like a housecat watching two drunken mice.

He cut an imposing image, tall with broad shoulders filling out a pristine navy double-breasted coat with polished gold buttons. It fell nearly to his ankles on matching trousers that were tucked neatly into his shiny black boots.

A guard, perhaps?

I resisted the urge to smooth down my unruly scarlet curls, for all the good it would have done, lifting my chin proudly instead.

The man's gaze moved to Davin.

"I see you've recovered." He spoke the common tongue, but his accent was harsh, with thick, rolling Rs and a guttural sound.

"You mean from your men drugging us?" Davin asked.

"I actually meant from the copious amounts of vodka you consumed, given that we found two empty bottles among the several you were smuggling." His eyebrows rose slightly, and I couldn't tell if he was mocking us or merely being matter of fact.

Probably the first one.

Still, at least he didn't seem to know who we were. It was only the vodka he was concerned about. *Surely, that's better.*

"We would recover better with some water." I forced myself to my feet, though the action made black spots appear in my vision.

6

He only gave me a cursory glance before addressing my cousin as though he were the one who spoke.

"Tell me what you were doing in the tunnels, and I might look into it."

I opened my mouth to respond, but Davin spoke first. "Tell us who you are first."

The man pursed his lips like he wanted to argue, then let out a short breath. "I am Lord Theodore Korhonan, brother to His Grace, Iiro Korhonan, Duke of Clan Elk."

Not just a guard, then.

"Well, Laird Theodore—" I began.

"It is Lord, here," he corrected, still mostly avoiding looking in my direction.

I blinked. *Lord* sounded ridiculous, but if that's what he wanted to be called... Davin made a face like he was biting back another laugh.

"Very well, *Lord Theodore.* As I'm sure you noticed, we were...procuring a few items that are difficult to find in Lochlann."

"Stealing," he clarified.

"Of course not," I answered. "We paid for it."

"Overpaid, at that," Davin added.

"And where did you plan to consume it?"

Davin and I exchanged a confused look. "At home. In Lochlann."

There was a tense silence before Lord Theodore spoke again, his voice a deep timbre echoing off the stone walls. "The punishment for stealing is losing a hand."

"I told you, we paid—" My words cut off abruptly when he finally turned the full force of his gaze on me.

Torchlight flickered in his golden green eyes, and for

7

the smallest fraction of a moment, pity broke through his stoicism. For the first time since we discovered our route home obliterated, I felt truly afraid.

His features hardened into resolve, though, as he finished his thought. "But the punishment for smuggling is death."

CHAPTER 2

M y blood froze in my veins, and I tried to force my foggy brain to work.

Lord Theodore took in my surprise, his face and tone devoid of emotion. "I take it you were not aware of this law."

Anger chased away the rest of my shock at his cavalier attitude toward something that would cost Davin and I our lives. I straightened to my full five feet, making sure to look down my nose at him even though he towered over me by a solid foot.

"No, I was not aware of this law, because in Lochlann we are not barbarians who execute people over a few bottles of booze."

A muscle in his square jaw ticked. "And in Socair, we do not wantonly break laws and oaths and believe there will be no consequences."

Clearly, they still blamed us for the war, just because my mother had helped her best friend out of a marriage pact with a Socairan duke twice her age.

9

Lord Theodore straightened like he was recovering himself, the hard mask taking over once more. "Regardless," he said, "the law is clear."

He spun on his heels to walk away, his solid boots clacking ominously against the gray stone floors like shiny harbingers of death.

I glanced at Davin. My cousin's face betrayed none of the fear or anxiety I knew he must be feeling, nor any accusation, even though meeting up with the smuggler had been my idea this time.

Whether he blamed me or not, I certainly did. I had to do something to get us out of this. It was a gamble, but things could hardly get worse than *punishable by death*.

"Wait!" I called after him, my voice echoing off of the dungeon walls.

I could see Davin's head shake slightly in the corner of my vision, but I ignored him. The lord came to a halt, turning slightly back toward me.

"Yes?" he asked.

"You introduced yourself, but I didn't."

He finished turning around, his posture rigid. "That's not—"

"I am Rowan Pendragon," I interrupted him. "Princess and second-in-line to the throne of Lochlann."

His full lips parted, and he shook his head wordlessly. Stepping closer to the iron bars, he looked me over, from the wild scarlet curls that hung in disarray around my face to the cream-colored dress that was filthy but made of fine crushed velvet.

He turned to look at Davin. "And you are her guard?"

I suppressed an unladylike snort.

Davin was decent with a sword, but I had been trained by my father and the formidable Lady Fia. Still, no need to make that obvious. They had taken my belted sword away, but I had my siren dagger holstered at my thigh. It would be easier to use if they didn't suspect I knew how.

"I am *Laird* Davin, Marquess of Lithlinglau, and first cousin to Princess Rowan," Davin responded, giving Lord Theodore a bow that was only slightly mocking.

A stilted silence followed Dav's statement. The Lord pressed his full lips together like he wasn't sure whether to curse or laugh.

"You expect me to believe that a marquess and a princess decided to risk their lives for...six bottles of vodka?"

When he put it that way...

"In our defense, it was very good vodka," Davin chimed in.

"Besides, there shouldn't have been a risk. We've been down that tunnel dozens..." I trailed off as I realized I was admitting to smuggling more than once, and Davin sighed.

"That doesn't explain what you were doing on the Socairan side."

"The cave-in blocked our exit back to Lochlann." Davin spoke up. "We had no choice—"

"The rubble that has been clear for a decade just happened to close when the two of you were inside?" The lord interrupted him, his tone laced with skepticism.

And again, he looked only to Davin, as though he were the only one capable of answering. I narrowed my eyes, though that only made Theodore's face swim in my vision.

"There was a storm." One I had sensed coming, but I never imagined it would hit with that magnitude.

"So, a tunnel under a mountain that has weathered thousands of storms, happened to cave in right when you were strolling through?" He shot me a dubious look.

I scoffed. "Now that you mention it, perhaps we simply decided to take a leisurely five-day stroll through the frozen tunnels with no water, no cloaks, and no supplies, to visit a kingdom who hates us."

"Indeed," Davin tacked on gravely. "A dastardly plan that only came to fruition when your soldiers drugged us and carted us away. Now we're just where we wanted to be, so thank you, kind sir, for playing right into our hands."

A small snort of laughter escaped me, and Davin smirked.

"You are lying." But doubt coated the lord's words.

I sighed, pulling out the chain around my neck with the signet ring even I wasn't stupid enough to leave home without.

The heavy gold seal had an embossed shield and sword, the symbol representing Lochlann. Carved into the shield was a tree with curling branches accented with leaves and berries. A rowan tree.

Theodore stared at it for a long moment before turning to walk away without a word, leaving me to wonder if telling him the truth about who I was had helped us at all.

Or was it only the latest misstep in my endless line of mistakes?

CHAPTER 3

Only when the lord was gone did I allow myself to sink back down to the cold stone ground, leaning my head against the equally frigid stone wall.

Davin slid close to me on the other side of the bars, his posture nearly as defeated as I felt.

"Do you think they'll actually kill us?" I asked.

He let out a slow breath. "I would like to think they wouldn't risk a war, but Socairans hold grudges. They may feel safe on their side of the mountain. And stars, Row, killing us is hardly the worst thing they could do. They could just leave us in this dungeon to freeze to death."

I dropped my voice. "As charming as staying in this dungeon sounds, at least it will be warmer tonight."

"That is a comfort. I love it when your woo-woo powers come in handy."

That was unusual enough. The most I could do with my basic weather intuition was tell someone when to pack an extra cloak. Still, Davin was the only one of my cousins or siblings without any fae blood, so he had always insisted it was "woo-woo."

"It's science, Dav, not magic." I whispered the familiar argument, laughing a little under my breath. "I'm just a little closer to nature than most people are. You know, like how you're a little closer to all the ladies of the court than most of the other lairds are."

He huffed out a laugh, returning to his usual glib demeanor. "Speaking of things I miss about Court, do you at least think the stuffy *lord* left to get lunch?"

"One can dream."

BUT WHEN LORD THEODORE RETURNED SEVERAL HOURS later, there was no food in sight.

I opened my mouth to comment on it, but closed it as he pulled a heavy iron key from his coat. He unlocked the door, swinging it open as he barked something in Socairan to someone I couldn't see.

Two hulking guards marched in, wearing uniforms similar to Lord Theodore's, only the buttons were black and theirs had matching flat-topped caps. Wordlessly, they hauled us to our feet and escorted us up the winding staircase.

"If you're going to kill us, can we at least eat first?" I rasped out, my mouth even drier than it was this morning. "I'm starving."

Maybe they were taking us to be hanged. Or to torture our kingdom's secrets out of us. Either way, my stomach flipped and my mind raced with each step, but I didn't want them to know that.

"I second this movement!" Davin chimed in. "No one should be sent to their deaths on empty stomachs."

If I thought that Lord Theodore didn't care for us, the guards made their disdain even more obvious. Rough hands squeezed my arms after my plea for food, all but dragging me the rest of the way up the stairs.

Theodore led the way down several long hallways while my much shorter legs scrambled to keep up, lest I give my guard another excuse to drag me. Finally, we stopped at a large open room with no furnishings.

It appeared to be an entryway of sorts, with a black domed ceiling looming high above us. Long navy banners hung on either side of the massive doorways, adding the only pop of color to the oppressively daunting room, and just above each of the three door frames were gargantuan brown antlers.

"I think I preferred the dungeons," Davin said once he was right next to me.

Though he was quiet, his voice carried through the spacious room, echoing off of the bare walls.

I nodded my agreement just as the door to our left groaned open, admitting a tall, dark-haired man in brocaded tawny robes. He surveyed us with a sharp, hawk-like expression.

The surrounding men dipped their heads in respect, but I held mine high.

"You two present quite the conundrum to me," the man said, his accent milder than Theodore's. "Imagine my surprise when I send my brother to patrol the tunnels for smugglers and he returns with Lochlannian royalty."

This must have been Iiro, the *Duke of Clan Elk*. His words hung in the air between us as I studied him. I would have known he was Theodore's brother even if no one had mentioned it.

His features were nearly identical, though the small lines around his hazel eyes and downturned mouth indicated he was in his early thirties. The only discernible difference between them was that where Theodore's hair was so light blonde, it was nearly white, Iiro's straight locks were deep brown.

"Sir Iiro, if we could explain—" I began.

"You will not address his grace without being spoken to," my guard stepped forward and hissed, interrupting me.

I snapped my mouth shut, though I didn't hide the aggravation burning from my eyes.

Lord Theodore stepped forward, raising a hand. "She is unfamiliar with our ways, Lev, and a princess." The authoritative arch of his features morphed to something more respectful when he turned to his brother. "Perhaps an exception could be made."

Sir Iiro's eyes narrowed as he looked between his brother and me, but he waved a hand. "You may speak."

How very gracious of him.

"As I was saying, we weren't smuggling to resell for profit. It was only a bit of vodka—"

"Only?" He cut me off with a condescending laugh. "Only a breach in the laws of your kingdom and mine. Laws I can hardly believe you were unaware of, if you are who you claim to be, as it was your father who banned trade between us to begin with."

I swallowed back guilt at the truth of his words. One more reason for Da' to kill me, if I managed to make it back alive.

"And I'm sure we will be amply punished for that in Lochlann, just as you would be amply compensated for our return," Davin spoke up. No one told *him* not to speak out of turn, confirming my suspicions about backward Socairan ways. "If you could arrange a way back to Lochlann for us, we would be very, very grateful."

Everyone laughed except for Lord Theodore.

"The mountain road is impassable for the season," he explained. "If what you say about the tunnels is true...there is no way back to Lochlann."

CHAPTER 4

There was no way home?

Panic rose up in my throat, but I swallowed it back down.

"For how long?" The words came out a croak, my voice still raspy from dehydration.

"At least six months, if there's an early spring," Lord Theodore said.

"Six months," I repeated through numb lips.

Half a year before I would see my family again. Half a year in the dungeons.

If they let us live that long.

Davin spoke up. "Could we not reside here for the time being, as..." he paused, "foreign dignitaries? And again, generous compensation will be arranged upon our safe return."

Lord Theodore exchanged a thoughtful look with his brother, who shook his head.

"If it were up to me alone, I could be persuaded in that

direction," Sir Iiro intoned in a somewhat bored voice. "I have no desire to incite a war."

I didn't dare to let myself hope, not when he was clearly about to qualify that statement. Sure enough, he went on.

"But you have broken Socairan law. Perhaps your own country would look the other way at your dishonorable behavior, but here we do not frivolously thwart our principles."

A few voices sounded around us in agreement, but Lord Theodore looked troubled. I tried to keep my features neutral.

"In any case," Sir Iiro said after a moment, "this is not our decision alone, as it will affect all of the clans. The Summit will decide your fate."

Well, that sounded ominous.

"Who or what is—" Davin began, but the duke cut him off with a gesture.

"I have business to attend to. We will reconvene for dinner," Iiro declared before turning to leave.

Pompous arse.

Lord Theodore came to first cut the lines on Davin's rope, then mine. I wanted to ask him more questions about the Summit, but I didn't want to reveal my concern. Fia's advice resounded in my head, something she said every time I winced when her sparring stick hit me.

To give your enemy a reaction is to give them power. Now I know where to hurt you.

Staring up into those guarded hazel eyes, I knew one thing for certain. Behind that beautiful facade, Theodore Korhonan was absolutely my enemy.

"So, no more friendship bracelets then?" I tilted my head to the side in mock disappointment. "And just when I thought we really had something special."

His jaw tightened, but he didn't react any more than that.

"This way," was all he said as he turned to exit the grand room.

Davin and I followed, both of us flexing our hands to get blood flowing back into them while we walked. Our cheery guards walked at our backs, in case we decided to make a run for it with our complete lack of food, water, and basic resources.

At least they gave us some breathing room this time. Perhaps Theodore's princess comment had struck a chord.

When we approached the turn that led to the dungeons, the lord surprised me by going left, leading us to a grand staircase winding up instead of the narrow set that led down.

"We're not going back to the dungeons?" I asked, moving to walk next to him.

"That isn't necessary anymore. You'll be staying in your own rooms now, as the dungeon is not a fit place for a *princess* to sleep."

"He said dubiously," I retorted, raising my eyebrows,

"You don't act like a princess."

Davin snorted behind me, but I only gave Theodore a bemused smile.

"No? Do you have much experience acting like a princess?"

His lips parted, in offense or surprise. "Obviously not."

"Then it would appear that between the two of us, I'm

21

the only one who knows how a princess behaves. I'm glad we have cleared that up." I looked over my shoulder at my cousin. "At least our cages will be more elegant now."

The lord stiffened in response. "Do you take nothing seriously? Is this all a joke to you?"

His question sounded oddly reminiscent of one my father had asked recently, but I refused to think about that.

"Do you take *everything* seriously?" I asked instead. "I'm surprised you even know what a joke is."

He narrowed his eyes, but continued on without response.

When we reached the end of the wide, empty hall, he showed me to one door while the guards led Davin to the next one over. My stomach twisted.

Though this appeared to be what Lord Theodore said it was, a guest room, in a far less intimidating section of the castle than they'd been kind enough to allow us to use before, I couldn't help the nervous knot in my stomach at being separated from my cousin.

Davin caught sight of my expression and gave me a subtle nod.

"I don't know about you, Row." He yawned loudly. "But I'm going to take a nap before dinner." The tension in my shoulders eased a bit.

His message was clear. We were safe. Safe for now, at least.

I nodded back to my cousin and turned to face the room in front of me.

Davin excelled at reading people and situations both. If he believed we were safe, then I trusted him. Besides, I supposed it didn't make sense that they would escort us to guest rooms only to kill us.

Lord Theodore gestured for me to enter a room as opulent as the rest of the estate. A roaring fire blazed in the hearth with a steaming bath just before it, and gold-and-cream paper lined the walls around a bed stacked high with furs and plush velvet pillows.

I took in the rest of the room, my eyes finally resting on a tray laden with fruits and biscuits and cheeses, along with a small kettle and cup for tea.

My stomach growled, and it took all the restraint I had not to dive face first into the tray and devour every last crumb.

"Now that you've seen the *elegant cage,* would you prefer the dungeon, instead?" Lord Theodore's voice burst the small bubble I'd momentarily been in.

Making a show of ruminating on the question, I finally shook my head.

"As cozy as the dungeons were, they had a distinct lack of biscuits."

The smallest tinge of amusement tempted the corner of his mouth, but it disappeared as he spun to leave. Just before he shut the door, he paused, turning back to me.

"You don't strike me as a lush." He phrased it as a question.

I blinked at the non sequitur. "Well, I didn't strike you as a princess, either."

Lord Theodore stared at me for a long moment before speaking again. "If you are who you say you are, then why did you take the risk of buying from a Socairan smuggler, just for a few bottles of vodka?"

If his tone had been judgmental like it was earlier, I would have ignored him completely, but there was nothing aside from genuine curiosity this time.

So I thought about that day. There were a thousand answers I could have given him, but for some reason, I found myself settling on something close to the truth.

"Because it's my sister's favorite drink."

CHAPTER 5

As soon as he shut the door behind him, I regretted my answer. Not because I cared what he thought, but because saying the words out loud made me think of my Avani.

And I couldn't afford to think of her right now, couldn't face the possibility that I might never see her again.

Taking a deep, calming breath, I tried to ease the tightness in my chest before heading toward the food tray.

My mother always told us life looked better on a full stomach. At the very least, it couldn't look much worse.

I was so thirsty that I downed a cup of the steaming tea first, ignoring the way it left a trail of liquid fire all the way down my throat. Just as I was pouring another one, there was a timid knock. Sighing, I set my cup down and went to open it, assuming the lord had forgotten something, and was surprised to find a young woman standing there instead.

She was several inches taller than me, with broad

shoulders and deep brown hair. Her red, boxy dress had puffy sleeves and a white apron over it that told me she was probably a maid of some sort.

A visible shudder went through her when her blue eyes landed on my hair, and she did something with her hand that I was fairly certain was meant to ward off evil.

"I help you bathe and dress," she said with a much thicker accent than Theodore's.

What I wanted was a moment alone to eat and collect myself, but I had no way of undoing the laces at the back of my gown without help. I had left my ladies maid behind in Hagail, and had been wearing this dress ever since.

Besides, there was no point in further offending our hosts when our lives apparently hung in the balance.

"I would be grateful for your assistance," I said, stepping back to allow her entrance.

She closed the door behind her, laying what appeared to be draperies on the foot of the bed, and gestured for me to turn around, still avoiding looking directly at me.

"What's your name?" I asked, trying to coax some conversation out of her.

"Venla." The word was clipped, effectively dissuading me from further conversation.

She made quick work of my laces, and my dress fell to my feet just in time for her to give a horrified gasp.

Surely it wasn't modesty, when she came in here with the intent of bathing me. My brow furrowed, and I turned to see her widened eyes fixed on the dagger sheathed at my thigh.

I wasn't sure if she was more scandalized by the fact

that I was armed or by the dagger itself, a golden, bare-chested siren carved with careful attention to detail.

"It's just an heirloom," I explained, but her wide eyes told me it made no difference to her.

With a sigh, I unbuckled the leather straps of the sheath, setting the whole thing close enough to be within grabbing distance, and climbed into the tub. The warm water seeped into my core, finally thawing my frozen center. I shivered, and slipped further down in the tub, grateful to finally be warm again.

The relaxation part of my bath was short-lived, however, when Venla came at me with a rough cloth, scrubbing my body as if it was caked in layers and layers of mud. When she got to my hair, there was a reproachful silence, a visible hesitation.

Was it the color she found so offensive, or were curls unusual here, too?

It wasn't in Lochlann, or at least, not in my family. I had four sisters, one older and three younger. Every one of them had the same fiery shade, though mine was by far the curliest.

For the first time since the cave-in, I allowed myself to think, really think, about my family.

My mother, the renowned Warrior Queen, and my father, the legendary war hero, who had reunited and rebuilt a kingdom all while raising five daughters.

They had already lost one child, their only son, the same week he was born.

My older sister Avani had married the love of her life only to lose him a year later, and the younger three girls were growing up in the shadow of death and grief and sadness.

What will this do to them?

No one knew where Davin and I had gone that day, not even my lady's maid. Would they assume we were dead, that the rebels who refused to be rooted out of Hagail had gotten ahold of us?

I thought about my father's plea not to do anything stupid, about Lord Theodore's question.

Why take the risk?

It hadn't seemed like a risk, not really. A tunnel that should have been stable, a smuggler we had dealt with a dozen times.

Yet, here we were.

"You get dressed now." Venla's blunt words pulled me from my thoughts, which was just as well.

What was done was done. All I could do now was focus on staying alive so that my family wouldn't have to grieve me in truth, and that left no time for sinking into despair.

As soon as I was dry, I fastened my dagger back to my thigh. Venla tracked the motion, but said nothing, only helped me into the heaps of fabric she had brought.

A cream-colored underdress connected from the high neck all the way down the front with tiny gold buttons. She struggled with the buttons around my bosom, muttering something under her breath that sounded suspiciously like a Socairan curse word.

Next came an emerald overcoat, the velvety fabric so heavy I nearly stumbled under the weight of it. She pulled it in so that it covered my chest, lacing it with a ribbon.

Despite the fabric being stiff and unwieldy, the dress would have been beautiful, were it not several inches too long. Venla shook her head, pulling out a needle and thread from her apron. I stood precariously still while she attacked the dress with quick, sharp stitches in a few targeted places, bringing the hem up enough that it only barely scraped the floor.

"Thank you, Venla," I told her sincerely.

It would have been beyond embarrassing to drag my skirts around like a child all evening.

Instead of responding, she wordlessly shot my hair a wary look, motioning for me to sit in the chair. I watched her work in the vanity mirror, noting the way she cringed as she attacked my curls.

After what felt like hours, she wrangled it into a version of the demure bun she was wearing, only mine was partially concealed by a tall headband resting in front of it, covered with cream and emerald fabric that accented the colors in the dress.

Even without my red curls, I would have stood out among these people. Where their skin was swarthy and rich, mine was fair, like my father's. And while Theodore and Iiro's eyes had been a deep, hazel shade of green, mine were bright spring green like my mother's.

I glanced back and forth between our reflections in the mirror and couldn't help but notice that while her bun was neat and functional, mine was...artfully unruly.

At least, I hoped that's what it looked like. Though I suspected it was closer to resembling one of the fancy strawberry cakes Cook always made back home.

The soft, impractical slippers she placed on my feet

served as the final confirmation of everything I had begun to suspect about Socair.

Like this dress that was impossible to move in, like these shoes that would crumple upon actual contact with the ground outside, women here were supposed to be ornamental. Quiet, demure, and unassuming.

Well, my father had always said I couldn't behave if my life depended on it. It looked like we were about to find out.

CHAPTER 6

W hen Venla finally left, demanding that I rest until Lord Theodore came to *fetch* me for dinner, I took my first real, deep breath.

A thousand and one thoughts ran through my mind, beginning with how the hell we were going to get out of this situation, and ending with every worst-case scenario I could imagine.

Taking one of the small biscuits from the tray of food, I slathered some honey and butter on it before popping it into my mouth. It had been days since I'd had anything fresh to eat, and I hoped that if I could sate my appetite, I would be able to think a little clearer.

I was wrong.

The sweet and savory dough melted across my tongue, momentarily making all thoughts disappear. All that existed for one single, beautiful moment was this biscuit.

There wasn't enough time to relish the bite in my mouth before my hands were coating the next several biscuits with butter and honey in preparation to shove them into my throat as quickly as possible.

My stomach growled in response, pleased with this course of action as the cycle was repeated, bite after each delicious bite.

I had a brief thought about whether or not the food was poisoned before I dismissed it entirely. Surely, they wouldn't go through all the trouble of bathing and dressing me just to end me with a biscuit...

Then again, if I was going to die, this would be a worthy last meal.

I polished off the remaining morsels from the tray and ate several of the apple slices with the thin, hard cheese on top, along with a couple of large, red grapes before forcing myself to stop.

Before this past week, that easily could have been the appetizer before my main course. After being deprived of a full meal for so long, though, I needed to be careful not to overexert my stomach.

However difficult of an idea that might be for me to accept.

Reluctantly, I moved away from the small table, dusting off any crumbs from my mouth and the bodice of my dress, before going to test the door handle.

A whisper of excitement ran through me when the handle didn't stick. *Unlocked, then.* I gently pulled the large oak door open far enough to peek out into the empty hallway. There were guards stationed farther down near the stairs, but none outside of my door or even looking this way.

Opening it wide enough to slip through, I closed it behind me, grateful for the silent hinges.

I should have stayed in my room. In fact, I debated going back for a whole three seconds before deciding to explore instead, telling myself it was progress to even consider doing the safer thing.

My feet guided me past Davin's door, and I wondered if I should stop to ask him to come with me until I heard the snores coming from inside his room. I rolled my eyes. He always had been able to sleep through anything.

So, I continued on, creeping further and further down the hall until I eventually found myself in an entirely different wing of the estate.

Things were so different here than in Lochlann. The castles back home were full of history and life. Loud children, nobles, or even servants filled the halls with sound while the walls themselves held relics from our past, my mother's favorite paintings, or vases full of flowers.

The Elk Estate felt solemn by comparison, with so few people wandering the halls, and no children or servants running around. It was eerily quiet, making me aware of the soft padding of my slippers against the navy carpets lining the hall.

Like the room where we first met Iiro, they offered the only real pop of color to the otherwise muted and dull atmosphere. Everywhere I looked, it was straight lines and spartan decor interspersed with one or two grand chandeliers or lanterns.

And it wasn't just the hallways. The rooms I happened to peek in on were the same way. Muted colors and minimalistic designs covered the furniture, walls and floors.

Glancing down at my dress and the bright fabrics, I had to wonder if everything was decorated sparsely so that the people stood out, so that *they* drew the eye instead.

With a shrug, I tucked that thought away and continued my secret exploring until a throat pointedly cleared behind me.

Stars.

"Princess Rowan."

I slowly turned around to face the lord and his expectant expression.

"Lord Theodore." I dipped my head in greeting, not offering an excuse for my exploration.

He returned the gesture, examining me from the hastily altered hem of my emerald dress up to the curls already stubbornly escaping my bun.

"Will I pass for a proper Socairan?" I asked, mostly to break the awkward silence.

He stiffened and cleared his throat again, his golden-green eyes failing to meet mine.

"Somehow I doubt proper is a word used to describe you often," he muttered, shaking his head. "Or Socairan, for that matter," he added with a pointed look at my hair.

"Ah yes, the telltale red hair. At least you aren't shuddering in revulsion like my maid did."

The corner of his mouth twitched in what might have been amusement, but he quickly smothered it. "After the stories of King Logan bringing down the mountain, many of the villagers believe that red hair is a curse."

Of course they did. "And you?"

He assessed me imperiously. "That remains to be seen."

I held his scrutinizing gaze with one of my own, noting the curiosity softening the arrogant set of his brows.

"Perhaps you can deliberate the issue while you show me around your estate," I prodded. Anything was better than going back to my rooms to be alone with my thoughts.

He cocked his head suspiciously before he sighed, relenting. "I suppose there's no harm in it, since you clearly can't be trusted to stay in your rooms."

"That's the spirit." I held out my hand expectantly until he reluctantly offered his arm and led me down the hallway.

The muscles were taut cords under my fingertips, his posture as rigid as it was when we were in the dungeons, and I had to wonder if the man ever relaxed.

I was taken aback when we rounded the corner. In contrast to the emptiness of the rest of the estate, this hall felt like an entire museum of Socairan history.

My eyes raked over the ornately decorated display cases and elegant portraits hanging on the walls. Theodore paused to let me take it all in, clearly proud of this section of his home.

The very picture of decorum, he pointed out things as we went, diamond-encrusted and bejeweled eggs in protective glass containers, statues that represented one clan leader or another.

The flags that Clan Elk had borne throughout the centuries, all with varying shades of navy surrounding tan elk antlers in the center. There was even a massive portrait of what I assumed to be a royal family, unless all of the clans wore crowns and tiaras. I raised my eyebrow in question, and he explained.

"That was the monarchy, before an assassin eradicated the entire line." He sounded more matter of fact than upset, but my jaw still dropped.

I knew from the few spies my parents sent into Socair that there was no longer a monarchy, but I had never heard this version of why.

"That's why there are clans now?" I looked up at him beneath a furrowed brow.

"There were always clans." He had a way of explaining things in a tone that said I should already know them. "They simply used to be united under a king. Now, all we do is sit around fighting each other for the right to a throne that the villagers believe is cursed anyway." He turned to leave the portrait, and I tried for a lighter tone.

"Is there anything the villagers don't believe is cursed?"

"Well, that depends on who you're asking." His tone was dry.

He led me around the corner, all the way down another hallway to a set of double doors that opened to the outside. At a gesture from him, the guards on either side swooped in to open them.

We stepped out onto a terrace, and my jaw dropped.

All this time, I had assumed we were right next to the mountains. For that matter, I had assumed most of Socair was mountainous, harsh and austere. Even though I had known the temperature itself was mild, the air clear and still, I didn't expect it to be beautiful.

But this estate was nestled in a sprawling valley, with miles of trees with autumn leaves every shade from deep crimson to bright, stunning yellow. The sun was setting, casting the valley in a golden glow that turned the leaves into flickering flames, dancing with the wind.

I stared past the trees to the mountains in the distance. It was disorienting, seeing the jagged peaks from this angle, a mirror image of what they should have been.

I had spent my entire life with the Masach Mountains on the western horizon, but they looked so foreign from this side, and somehow even more daunting.

My heart plummeted into my stomach then as it hit me just how far away from home I was.

And that I might never see it again.

CHAPTER 7

Our trek to dinner was filled with the same polite sort of conversation. As we approached the dining hall, however, it quickly dampened into an oppressive silence, reminding me once again how different Socair was from home.

In Lochlann, the noise from the table alerted you to the meal even more than the savory smells floating in the air. That was most definitely not the case here. Though the table was filled, no one spoke.

There was no out-of-turn stealing of a roll from the bread basket or chatter about the happenings of the day.

It was only silence and waiting.

"Princess Rowan, how nice of you to join us," Iiro finally said from his seat at the head of the table, his words echoing in the quiet space.

Theodore flushed with shame, and I gathered that we had dawdled too long.

"The pleasure is mine," I said in a bland tone, pretending I didn't know that he was displeased.

ROBIN D. MAHLE & ELLE MADISON

A muscle in his jaw ticked, and the room fell into another uncomfortable silence.

A gorgeous woman sat to Iiro's left, dressed in clothes similar to mine, only hers were shades of blue and white and silver.

Davin sat on her other side, and when he met my eye, it was easy to see he was just as baffled by the awkward atmosphere as I was. I kept silent, though, as Lord Theodore showed me to a chair directly across from him, before taking the seat between me and the duke.

The man on my right shot me the horrified glance I was coming to expect and scooted his chair several inches away. I noticed with some irritation that the woman in red, on the other side of Davin seemed to have no such compunctions, shooting him coy glances that he returned in kind.

As soon as we were all settled, Iiro raised a hand and the maids around the room jolted forward, making quick and efficient work of serving each person seated.

Iiro made a gesture in the air. As if on cue, a gentle hum of conversation began, most of it in Socairan.

"This is my wife, Inessa," Sir Iiro gestured to the woman at his side.

Her hair was pale like Theodore's, though her eyebrows were several shades darker, hanging low over deep-set brown eyes.

"Welcome." Her voice was polite, but forced, and I wondered what I had already done to offend her, or if it was just my presence and hair that did the trick.

One of the maids stepped up behind me, ladling a bright red soup into my bowl. A pungent, tangy odor drifted up from the bowl, and I warily tried to identify the contents.

"It's borscht," Theodore offered in his usual high-handed tone. "Beet soup."

We had beets in Lochlann, but only ever served them with salads or as a side dish, so this meal was wholly strange to me. Dipping my spoon into the bowl, I took a discreet sniff before tasting it, and immediately regretted it.

At closer range, the cloying scent of vinegar stung my eyes, and I tried to blink it away. The entire table seemed to be observing me, so I quashed my hesitation, lifting the spoon to my lips and tilting the contents into my mouth

I nearly spit it back out.

It was cold, for one thing. *Why?* Why was soup cold in the middle of autumn? And how did it taste even worse than it smelled?

"Mmm," I said, trying not to cringe at the sour aftertaste.

Perhaps the slimy concoction would have been better if I hadn't smelled it, or if it had been warm. Or perhaps it was always going to taste like vinegar and dirt.

Either way, I felt the eyes of both Iiro and his brother on me, like my reaction was some sort of test.

I refused to let them know how disgusting I found it, then steeled my features into neutrality while forcing my hand to dip the spoon and bring it to my lips once more.

"How do you like it?" Duke Iiro asked, though his features told me he knew perfectly well how I liked it.

"It's quite..." I cut off with a cough, the vile soup in the back of my throat threatening to resurface.

"Delicious." Davin broke in before I could lie badly, his tone overly polite. "We don't have this in Lochlann."

Something I'm grateful for.

I shot him an appreciative glance and the corner of his mouth tugged up in response.

Iiro muttered something noncommittal in response, and the scrutiny seemed to be lifted from me, at least for a little while.

Whatever was next smelled tantalizing and completely beet-less, and I found my mouth watering as the servants presented us with the next course. The steel domes over the dishes were removed to reveal noodles and hunks of beef in a creamy gravy.

Much better.

Just as I was about to take a bite, Theodore cleared his throat.

"Stroganoff," he intoned, just as stiff as before. "You eat it with the large fork."

I was tempted to continue using the small fork just to see if he would actually die from the breach of propriety, but I dutifully plucked up the larger one. The dish looked and smelled delicious enough that I didn't really care how it was eaten.

It was an effort not to groan with pleasure as I took my first bite. The gravy-soaked beef practically melted in my mouth, and I knew then that it would take more than a few dirty glances to keep me from licking the plate when I was finished.

I had just taken a second bite of the divine noodles when Davin's voice rang out. "Sir Iiro, perhaps you would like to tell us more about this Summit now."

Ever the diplomat.

Iiro nodded once in his brother's direction, a sharp dip of his head.

"As you may know, there are nine clans in Socair," Theodore began. "Since the monarchy was destroyed, the clans have operated independently, but there are still a very few laws which we all adhere to for the sake of order. When something comes up that affects all of the clans, a Summit is called in neutral territory."

"I have already alerted my closest allies to your presence, as well as sent messenger birds to the other clans with a summoning," Iiro added. "They will decide what happens to you."

"You mean, whether we're ransomed or set free?" I asked hopefully.

"I mean whether you live or die," Iiro corrected.

Logically, I had been expecting that, but the indifference in his tone had blood rushing in my ears, the roaring noise drowning out whatever Davin said in response. I stared at my cousin, suddenly more terrified than I had ever been in my life. It was my fault he was here, and it would be my fault if he died.

I toyed with an idea I had been chewing on in the back of my mind, convincing myself it would work. The rest of the table was conversing, even Theodore and Iiro discussing something with their heads close.

I nudged Davin's foot under the table, and he turned his attention to me.

"Did anyone announce you?" I asked in a low tone.

"No. *I* was on time," he teased. "Speaking of which, what were you and Lord *Theodore* up to?"

"He was giving me a tour."

"Of what?" He raised his eyebrows to convey his meaning, and I scowled at him, glancing around to make sure no one was paying attention.

"So no one has mentioned...who you are?" I barely mouthed the last words.

He shot me a quizzical look, but answered. "No, no one has spoken to me."

Perfect.

I turned to Iiro.

"Did you tell the clans why you were gathering them?" I asked, interrupting the duke as he spoke to his brother. "Did you tell them we were here?"

Inessa looked appalled, but I ignored her, staring directly at the man in charge.

Iiro narrowed his eyes at me before answering. "No." He glanced pointedly around the room. "Though, I daresay your presence won't remain a secret for long."

I nodded slowly, taking a deep, steadying breath.

"Of course. I have to go answer for my...deeply heinous crimes. But, Davin..." I let the idea hang in the air. I wasn't worried about the name. It was common enough in Lochlann, and I doubted the Socairans were familiar with every member of the extended royal family.

Iiro looked intrigued, but my cousin only looked horrified, like he suspected exactly what I was about to do.

"Rowan, no." Davin's words were a warning I ignored.

"When we were in the dungeons, Lord Theodore astutely noted that my companion was merely my guard. Surely, a nonroyal citizen, someone of no importance or rank—" I cut off when a foot connected solidly with my shin.

Barely suppressing a wince, I went on.

"Surely someone like that would be well within your own authority, you being such a powerful duke of a vast territory such as this."

Iiro's expression told me he knew I was flattering him, but he appeared to be considering it, nonetheless. I didn't breathe, hardly dared to hope, until, miraculously, he gave a slow nod.

"Your *guard* would have no need to be seen by the Summit, especially provided you remain amicable and accommodating."

Ah. That explained why he even considered it.

"Absolutely not," Davin said sharply. "It was both of our—"

"No." I cut him off with a sharp look. "This is my decision. I outrank you, Davin."

Not once in the seventeen years I had been alive had I pulled rank on my older cousin, but this was about his life. He opened his mouth to argue, and I held up a hand to stop him.

"You swore fealty to my family."

"Yes," he said through clenched teeth. "I swore to protect—"

"You swore to *obey*," I corrected. "And I'm certain you wouldn't want to break that oath, certainly not here, in front of our new friends."

Davin's eyes glowed with more fury than I had ever seen in them, but he clamped his jaw shut.

"As you say, Your Highness," he gritted out.

"Now," I turned back to Iiro, changing the subject intentionally. "I assume I'll want to prepare a statement of some sort, to explain—"

"My dear," Iiro cut me off. "You won't be speaking to the Summit. It is only because of your station and your unfamiliarity with our ways that you have been permitted to speak your case here, at this table."

I blinked. Surely, he was joking. I had assumed Inessa's sour looks were because I was from Lochlann, but now I wondered if she was merely offended that I had the audacity to speak at all.

Iiro went on before I could form a response, which was probably just as well.

"Even if you were Socairan, and a man, you could not make your own case before the clan leaders." His words were edged with condescension, as if that were painfully obvious.

"My brother will speak on your behalf," Theodore offered, and Iiro nodded like that, too, had been a given.

"That's very...gracious of you."

What else could I say, really, when he held both of our lives in his hands?

CHAPTER 8

I t was a long, tense walk back to our rooms.

Theodore had left dinner a few minutes early, asking one of the guards to escort Davin and me back. We had left not long after, the oppression of Davin's fury and my forthcoming judgment at the Summit proving to be even less pleasant company than Sir Iiro was.

Davin wordlessly entered his room and I headed for mine, but Lord Theodore's hesitant voice reached me just as I placed a hand on my door handle.

"Princess."

I paused, not especially in the mood for his thinly veiled pretension. My head was throbbing from the events of the day and the substantial weight of my hair piled up on top of it.

Having little choice, though, I turned slowly to face Theodore, trying to rein in my maelstrom of emotions.

"Your things." He thrust a satchel into my arms.

My satchel.

I took the bundle from him, noting that it was only

half of what I had been missing when I woke up, not including the vodka. "Where is my sword?"

"We protect our women in Socair." There was a clear implication that the men of Lochlann were lacking. "They have no need to wear weapons."

"So all the big strong men will fall all over themselves protecting me if the Summit decides to kill me?"

"If the Summit decides to put you to death, one sword won't be enough to change things." He spoke with no malice, but his matter-of-fact tone was worse, somehow.

I squeezed my eyes shut against the sudden panic threatening to overtake me. "Is this really the only way? Can't you just...quietly let us go?" It was as close to pleading as I had come, as close as I would come, but when I opened my eyes, he was shaking his head.

"The other clans would find out, and there would be blood in the streets. My brother has already been lenient with you," he added, somewhat defensively, with a glance toward Davin's door. "There will be a fair trial."

I knew I was pushing my luck after what Iiro was doing for my cousin, but my mouth hadn't yet caught up with my brain.

"I would hardly call a council of people who hate me and refuse to give me the chance to speak on my own behalf a trial, let alone a fair one," I scoffed, bitterness lacing my tone.

"What exactly did you expect to happen when you came here?" There was a trace of exasperation in his voice, enough to have my spine stiffening.

But his question was valid. What had I expected?

Was I really surprised that death was on the table

when the Socairans hated us? *No.* I had known that was a possibility from the moment the tunnel caved in.

Maybe the problem was that I had expected the Socairans to feel a lot more like enemies than they did right now. I hadn't expected to have a meal with them, to talk to them or tease them.

I hadn't expected to understand them, and somehow, that was worse.

"I don't know," I answered him at last, opening the door to my room and stepping inside. "Not this."

THIS TIME, I EXPECTED THE KNOCK ON THE DOOR.

I was halfway across the floor before the familiar *tap-tap-tap* was even finished. I opened the door to find Davin on the other side, just like I knew he would be.

"You can't do this." He pushed into my room, shutting the door behind him.

It was a mark of how upset he was that he didn't comment on the frilly, ruffled, high-necked monstrosity of a nightgown Venla had shoved me into.

"I can, and I have," I countered. I had spent the entire half hour Venla was pulling pins out of hair preparing for this conversation, so my voice was a calm contrast to the uncharacteristic heat in his. "I should never have dragged you into this."

"This is ridiculous. We have been in that tunnel a dozen times, and I have arranged at least half of them. I am no less culpable than you are, and you know it."

I let out a long, slow breath. "Be that as it may, they

already knew who I was. There is no getting out of this for me, but what would be ridiculous is for us both to go when only one of us has to."

Davin scowled. "Look me in the eye and tell me that if the tables were turned, you would let me go alone."

"If the tables were turned, I would know you wanted someone to tell our families what happened! The Socairans could kill us and never breathe a word of it, and our parents would never know what became of us." My voice broke. "I did this for all of our sakes."

"I'm not going home, though. I'm just here as leverage."

"Better leverage than dead," I shot back.

He got quiet then, and I took advantage of his silence to press a different point.

"There's still a vote, and you said yourself they have more to gain by keeping us alive. That's true. But if the worst does happen, there's no reason for our families to suffer both our losses, for your mother to suffer the way mine did when she lost her only son." I let that linger in the air before adding, "The way we all did when we lost Mac."

The name came out a whisper, and Davin winced. In the months since my sister's husband had died, we rarely mentioned him. He had been a part of our family since before I was born, and his death had taken a toll on every one of us.

Davin knew as well as I did that our families couldn't withstand one more, let alone two.

There was a stilted pause. "That's a low blow."

"It's the truth, though."

Davin deflated, like the fight had completely left him.

"I hate this," he said, running a hand through his hair.

"I know."

Crossing to the small cream-colored sofa by the window, he sank down with a sigh and made himself comfortable. When I raised my eyebrow, he shrugged.

"I'm not going to leave you without protection." There was a forced lightness to his tone, and I responded in kind.

"You didn't want to spend any more time alone, you mean."

In spite of being an only child, he never had gotten used to being solitary.

"Please," he scoffed. "Like I spent this afternoon alone."

I squeezed my eyes shut. "I hope you're joking, since we're already in enough trouble."

"Then let's say yes. Speaking of being in enough trouble, are you sure you don't want to try making a run for it?"

Shaking my head, I walked to the decanter on my side table, which I had been amused to discover was vodka.

If Theodore possessed a sense of humor, I would think he had sent it up as a joke, but it was probably just standard courtesy. Still, I wasn't complaining.

"You mean since we have so many friends here and I blend in so well with the Socairans?" I filled up both golden goblets, handing him his.

"Damn that cursed hair of yours."

I groaned, sitting next to him. "Who told you about that?"

"The lady friend I most definitely did not have in my

room earlier. She practically inspected my roots before she would consent to keep me company."

"I see," I said, shaking my head. "Well, regardless, we have little hope of help amongst the clans. No food. No supplies. Very little gold. Besides which, the pass is closed, so we have no way home, unless you want to take our chances on the tunnel again."

"I think I'd rather us both face the dubious justice of the Socairans than set foot in that stars-blasted tunnel ever again, certainly not just to starve to death when we reach the other side." He took a sip of his drink.

I raised my glass in salute. "Dubious justice of the Socairans, it is."

CHAPTER 9

Venla was thirty minutes into getting me dressed and had only used two of her signs to ward off the evil of my hair when someone knocked at the door. Assuming it was Davin, I called out for him to enter and was surprised to see the duke's brother there instead.

"Good morning, Lord Theodore," I greeted, before Venla roughly directed my face back toward the mirror.

"Good morning, Princess," he replied after a moment, his voice sounding a little uncertain. "I came to fetch you for breakfast, but..." He trailed off, and I felt more than saw him watching me.

Venla finished tying off the last ribbon in my hair, doing a far better job of keeping my long curls at bay today by allowing the lower half to flow freely down my back. As a bonus, my skull wasn't pounding from the strain like it had yesterday.

"But?" I asked.

Theodore cleared his throat and shook his head slightly.

"But, I'd hate to tear you away...from all the fun you're having."

I huffed a small laugh and glanced up at him to see if he was being serious. Spending time in Venla's company was far from anything I would consider *fun*.

"Indeed. I'm not sure I could be pulled away from such a joyous start to my day."

If I thought Theodore could laugh, I might have imagined that he chuckled in response. But that would be ludicrous.

"Speaking of joyous starts to the day, I thought I would have to drag you out of bed kicking and screaming this morning," he replied in his thick accent.

"You'd enjoy that, wouldn't you?" I fired back.

Venla gave one of her signature scandalized gasps, but Theodore only squeezed his eyes shut in exasperation.

"I only meant that you seemed unhappy last night."

"Well, my fate has not yet been sealed. There is still time to convince this Summit that I am infinitely better alive." I sighed. "And, if I'm bound for the gallows, I hardly want to spend my final days sulking in my room. I would rather *live* while I still can."

Theodore's head tilted ever so slightly to the side, bafflement widening his bright hazel eyes.

Venla muttered something under her breath and turned to face him. They spoke briefly in Socairan before she dipped into a curtsy and left, making sure to leave the door open wide as she went.

I looked after her with a rueful shake of my head. "I believe you mentioned breakfast?"

THIS TIME, WE DIDN'T GO TO THE LARGE DINING HALL.

Instead, Lord Theodore took me down the hall we had toured yesterday to a bright and airy room. A small, circular table sat near a bay window overlooking the grounds below.

Once again, the autumn trees were on display in their full glory, sparkling under the morning sun. Even without my extra awareness of the weather, it was clear the day was going to be perfect.

A pang went through me when I thought of the Autumn Festival back home. It was my favorite one of the year, full of sticky, candy-colored apples and pumpkin bread my mother spent days with us baking for the whole village. Every year, the farmers had a contest to see who could create the best maze through their cornfields.

No matter which way things here went, there was no way we would be at that festival this year.

A servant pulled a chair out for me at the table. The sound of the heavy wood scraping against the stone floor made me reluctantly tear my eyes away from the window long enough to take my seat.

Soon after we sat down, Davin joined us, followed by Iiro and Inessa. Despite the more intimate group, our meal was once again a somber affair. Especially since none of the delicious biscuits from the day before were present.

However, Theodore somehow managed to refrain from

55

telling me to use my only spoon to eat my dark, tasteless porridge, so I supposed that was an improvement.

Halfway through breakfast, a servant approached and leaned down to quietly speak to Theodore in Socairan. The lord nodded noncommittally until the last thing the servant said made his lips twist in distaste.

"All of the birds have returned with affirmations," he said to his brother, once the servant walked away. "Except for Bear, who merely thanks us for the invitation."

The duke rubbed his temple and sighed. "Must they always be difficult?" He gestured irritably for the next course. "Regardless, all that matters is that they received it. Even *they* can't refuse a summons to the Summit."

"I'm sure that rankles at them," Theo said. "You know how the duke is."

"And Evander is even worse," Iiro muttered.

Theodore nodded, his jaw clenched.

Davin and I exchanged a look, but no one expounded on that. Breakfast resumed in the same tense silence with which it had begun.

Once the dishes had been cleared from the table, Lord Iiro addressed his brother.

"Theo, you will keep an eye on our guests today while I prepare the convoy."

"Theo?" I asked before the lord could respond.

His shoulders stiffened, and a hint of red crept into his cheeks.

"Lord Theodore is fine," he responded flatly.

"Lord Theo it is." I beamed at him, causing a muscle in his jaw to twitch.

Iiro made a show of scratching his beard, but it was clear that he was hiding a smile behind his hand.

"So?" he pressed.

"Of course, Your Grace. I would...love to." *Theo*'s features said otherwise, but his brother didn't comment on it.

"Excellent," Iiro said.

"Excellent," Davin echoed, with a wide grin, his mood having improved somewhat from yesterday.

Inessa, of course, said nothing.

Excellent, indeed.

CHAPTER 10

"So, *Lord Theo,* what does keeping an eye on us entail?" I asked once breakfast was finally over, and Iiro and Inessa had left the room.

He pursed his full lips, but had stopped trying to get me to stop using the name after the seventh time I declined.

"I thought we could do something fun, but it would appear you are already enjoying yourself too much."

"Fun? I wasn't aware that Socairans knew the meaning of the word," I responded dryly.

"It might not be as enjoyable as annoying me or smuggling vodka, but then again, what is?"

A laugh escaped me. Perhaps he possessed a sense of humor, after all.

"Quite right, My Lord," Davin chimed in with his most pompous voice.

If Theo realized my cousin was mocking him, he didn't comment.

He reluctantly led us out of the breakfast room to an

59

outdoor courtyard. As uncomfortable and stiff as the dresses here could be, they did at least offer protection from the wind.

The temperature was mild, but every once in a while, a gust of icy wind would roll off the mountain. My dress was completely unfazed, standing as rigid as a stone wall while it blocked even the most determined of breezes.

About a third of the way down the vast courtyard were sets of small cylinders arranged in different patterns. It was unusual decor, but then, not much about the Socairans felt familiar.

Theo followed my gaze, taking note of my confused expression, and the corner of his lips tilted up.

"It's for the game, Gorodki." He picked up a wooden stick, gesturing toward the cylinders. "Those pins are the cities, and the goal is to banish them, like this,"

He threw the stick, taking out two of the structures, sending the pins scattering in different directions. Several servants scuttled over to stand them up again.

He handed Davin another stick, and my cousin stepped up to take his turn.

"Why am I not surprised that your idea of fun involves destroying a small town?" I commented.

Theo actually laughed, a deep and rich sound that made warmth flood through my chest, before he thought better of it and abruptly stopped.

"Are you and your cousin promised?" He looked like he wanted to take the words back as soon as he said them, and I wondered if he was only upset to have caught himself being conversational.

I nearly laughed out loud at his question, though.

Davin would only settle down when he was absolutely forced to, and I— catching Theodore's expression, I realized I had misinterpreted what he was asking.

"To each other?" I couldn't keep the disgust from my tone.

The assumption shouldn't have caught me off guard. It was common enough for cousins to marry most places. It had been in Lochlann, too, until a few years ago, but we had abandoned that tradition. Thankfully.

Davin was almost too attractive for his own good, with his black hair and bright blue eyes, but that would be like marrying my brother.

Theo nodded even more stiffly than usual. Maybe cousins didn't marry here, either, and that's why he looked so uncomfortable about it.

"No," I answered quickly. "No, not—no. Just no."

His shoulders seemed to relax a little.

"Neither of us is promised to anyone." I wasn't sure why I offered that last bit of information.

"I suppose your family doesn't have a good history with betrothals." The twitch of Theo's lips was the only sign that he might be joking rather than outright insulting.

Then the sound of Davin's stick clanging against the side of the castle pulled Theo's attention away from me and, fortunately, this conversation. Shaking his head, he walked over to help my cousin, leaving me with my thoughts.

He hadn't been wrong. My family didn't have a good history with betrothals. That had been one of the last things my mother and I argued about.

"Don't you know what I would have given for choices at your

age, what heartache and bloodshed might have been avoided if your father and I had been given any?"

When I didn't respond, my mother huffed out a breath. "If you don't choose someone, the council will choose for you."

"Then let them. Honestly, Mother, as long as he's not too old, what difference does it make?"

She ran a frustrated hand through her deep brown waves, spring-green eyes widening in disbelief. "What difference does it make?" she repeated. "We wanted to give you a chance at love, or at least the potential for it."

"What, so I could end up like Avani?" I had barely left my sister's side in weeks, but when I did, the sound of her sobs followed me down the hallway, echoing off the walls.

"Rowan..." My mother's features softened, and somehow her sympathy was worse than aggravation. It needled at a part of myself I didn't want to examine any more.

"It's fine," I muttered, getting to my feet. "Just choose someone who benefits the kingdom. One person starting a war for marriage is more than enough for this family."

A few days later, I had left for my ill-fated visit to Hagail, and now all I could see was my mother's stricken face as I walked away. It hadn't been fair of me, when there were so many reasons around that war and most of them had nothing to do with something so simple as marriage.

Still, I loved my parents together, but I didn't want the kind of love you went to war for.

I didn't want the kind of love that could break you.

CHAPTER 11

A few hours later, Theo escorted us to our rooms with the assurance our meals would be sent up since everyone was preparing to leave the next morning.

At least we wouldn't have to sit through another awkward dinner. Still, a solid knot formed in my stomach.

Leaving. Tomorrow. To entrust my fate to a group of men who hated me on principle.

I was so tired of stewing in my thoughts, I was almost grateful when Venla arrived, bringing with her a small meal of salted fish and boiled potatoes. After I ate under her watchful, disapproving eye, she dressed me in another charming nightgown before taking her leave.

The thick, ruffled fabric was tight against my neck, the color a pale pink that clashed marvelously with my hair.

Is this what they require all of their women to wear, or is it only me that has the pleasure? I imagined my sisters' faces if they saw—

A knock on the door effectively cut off that line of

thought, for which I was immensely grateful. I couldn't afford to think about my family if I wanted to get through this.

It was Davin, of course. When he came in, though, there was none of our usual easy conversation, not even yelling this time. We looked at each other like neither of us could quite decide what to say.

"If you get home before I do," I finally began.

"You mean if you don't get home at all," he countered.

"Details." I waved a hand, trying and failing for an air of casualness. "Regardless, tell my father...tell him I'm sorry he was right about me not being able to go five minutes without doing something stupid, but I hope I've finally done something smart."

Davin closed his eyes for several seconds as his fists clenched at his sides.

"If I get home *before* you, I won't be able to tell your father anything before he kills me for leaving you here."

"He'll understand," I insisted.

And I believed it. I wanted to think that my father would have made the same choice in my situation, even if he never would have intentionally landed himself here to begin with.

"Will he?" Davin demanded. "Because I'm not sure I do."

I hadn't seen him this serious since Mac died, and the sight nearly broke me.

"I don't have a choice. You know that." I looked away from him.

"And what's my choice, when I have to tell our families I stayed here safe while you traipsed off to die?"

"Don't be so dramatic," I chided in a tone far more confident than I felt. "We both know they're more likely to ransom me than anything. I'll probably be back here with you before you can even make the journey home." *I hoped.*

The corner of Davin's mouth twitched in a reluctant smile, and his shoulders began to relax a little.

"You had better be. You know you're my favorite cousin. It would be boring without you."

"You mean the others won't break all the rules with you?" I laughed, but quickly sobered when I remembered that our latest stint of rule-breaking had landed us here. "Perhaps that's for the best. Someone should keep you in line."

"Don't say that." He visibly shuddered. "I'd rather face the Socairan Summit than be boring for the rest of my life."

I managed a small smile. "Well, we all have to make sacrifices."

Instead of laughing at my off-color joke like he usually would, Davin surprised me by wrapping his arms around me.

"Remember, *Tellus Amat Fortis*." It was my family's motto. The world loves the strong. "And you are certainly one of the strong ones."

Then he pulled back, giving me a once over. "Even if you are wearing the most ridiculous nightgown I've ever seen."

I laughed. "Well, I'm sorry you feel that way since I had Venla fetch an extra one for you in blue, and it would mean the world to me if you put it on. You wouldn't deny me my dying wish, would you?"

"Psssh. You just said you weren't going anywhere, cousin, and I'm going to hold you to it." A mischievous glint appeared in his eyes. "But I tell you what, when you come back here alive, I'll wear one of these nightgowns in your honor."

"Well, then. That's all the incentive I need."

With that, we both broke into laughter.

I never thought I would be grateful for the clothing here, but that was all we needed to lighten the mood. After that, we spent the rest of the evening reminiscing and talking and doing everything but talk about the fact that I was leaving in the morning.

CHAPTER 12

As the carriage rolled away, I took one last glance through the window to see my cousin.

Davin's arms were crossed and his features were pinched. I knew Iiro insisted he stay behind so I wouldn't be tempted to run off, but I was grateful for it all the same.

If I was heading to my death, that wasn't something I wanted him to see.

I wanted him to remember me like I was last night, and I sure as stars didn't want him to do something stupid and get himself killed right along with me.

The massive carriage jostled and creaked more and more as we pulled further away from the castle. The roads went from being smooth and even, to dipping in and out in a more rugged terrain.

Everywhere I looked, there were villages nestled into hillsides, small farms that looked more brown than green. The crisp colors of autumn were on full display on the many trees, casting everything in red and gold hues.

ROBIN D. MAHLE & ELLE MADISON

Though we were a mountain pass away from home, this place felt like an entirely different world.

"So," I began, turning away from the window and breaking the silence of the small space. "Tell me about this Summit."

Duke Iiro raised his eyebrows imperiously, but he did eventually lower himself to explain.

"The leaders of all nine clans will convene on neutral territory to decide your fate, as we discussed before. Now, some of them are our allies." He nodded in his wife's direction. "We have a marriage alliance with Viper, and they with Eagle. They will likely side with me, though nothing is certain where Lochlann is concerned. Socairans have long memories, and resentment of your people runs deep."

I bit my tongue to refrain from mentioning that it was they who had invaded us.

"Lynx and Ram are mostly neutral. They rarely let anyone influence their votes. It is Bear that offers the most difficulty," Iiro went on. "They are the largest, and are allied with Crane and Wolf and have recently been in talks with Bison as well. They are our biggest threat."

Theo cleared his throat across from me, and Iiro nodded for him to speak.

"Do you truly believe that Duke Aleksandar would vote against her when he himself has a Lochlann bride?"

I glanced sharply at him, though I wasn't sure why that bit of news surprised me. Before the war, it must have been common to marry into Socair. It just hadn't been done in my lifetime.

"Aleksander would side against us just to spite us."

Iiro's eyes narrowed. "And you know Evander would do the same. He is just like his father."

Theo looked thoughtful, maybe even disappointed, and I couldn't resist the urge to needle at him. It was as good a distraction as any.

"Who ever would want to spite someone as charming and affable as the two of you?" My expression was politely interested.

A sharp gasp rang out from Inessa, and Theo raised his eyes skyward.

"Well, she isn't winning anyone's favor like this," he muttered.

"*She* is right here," I reminded him.

"*She* doesn't know when to remain silent." Theo looked at me pointedly.

I opened my mouth to respond, even knowing it would prove him right, but Iiro cut in sharply. "Then *she* can take the next several days on the road to learn how to behave as a proper Socairan woman. After all, I wouldn't like anyone to be embarrassed at the Summit." He finally turned to address me. "What do you say, Princess Rowan? Can you be as amicable and accommodating as you swore to be?"

I bristled at the not-so-subtle reminder of Davin's life being in his hands, and nodded.

"Of course, Sir Iiro. I can be a great many things." I smiled sweetly.

Iiro glared at me, and Theo held out a hand. "There is still time, Brother. I'm sure she will have gotten this out of her system by the time we get there." He shot me a warning glance.

"I am trusting you to make sure of it." Iiro glared at

me, but his words were for his brother. "I will be busy with the Summit, so her behavior will be your responsibility."

"I will see that she's ready," Theo said, his tone brooking no argument. He turned to me. "Right, Princess Rowan?"

"Of course," I said again, my tone on the sarcastic side of *demure*.

I turned to stare out the window once again, mostly to hide my irritable expression. Just past the guards on our side of the carriage, a family walked along the roadside.

When the mother caught sight of my hair, she stepped backward, pushing her child behind her and making the same sign Venla had to ward off evil.

Theo sighed, yanking the curtain closed and cutting off their view.

"And we'll need to cover her hair."

CHAPTER 13

The sun was beginning to set when we pulled off at a small village. The carriage slowed and finally came to a full stop on a wide road with rows of small houses and shops on either side.

"Why are we stopping so soon?" I asked as Iiro exited the carriage with Inessa following just behind him.

The duke shot his brother a pointed glance, and Theo sighed before looking at me. "Traveling at night is dangerous with the Unclanned roaming about."

"The Unclanned?"

"Those cast out of their own clans," he explained.

"So if you cut off a hand for stealing and a head for smuggling, what rates being cast out of your clans? Something in the middle?"

"No," he said darkly. "Those who are put to death are given an honorable burial, and their families are safe. The Unclanned bring dishonor to their family. It is much worse." He cut off my next question by stepping out of the carriage and extending a reluctant hand to help me down.

A part of me didn't want to take it, just to spite him, but Iiro's words from before had been clear. I needed to fall into whatever feminine Socairan line they expected of me if I wanted to protect my cousin and have a chance at winning the Summit over.

Placing my hand in Theo's, I stepped out of the carriage and onto the road. He surprised me by not letting me go when I attempted to pull away. Instead, he wrapped my hand inside of his arm to escort me down the street.

The tension emanating off of him made it clear this was not his choice, but instead of being irritated by that fact, I leaned into him, wrapping my other hand around his wide bicep as I saw a few of the other ladies doing with the gentlemen next to them.

"I can see that you take your training seriously, Lord Theodore." I gave his muscle a little squeeze.

Red crept up into his cheeks, and I found myself grinning wildly in response. A blush was more reaction than I could have hoped for.

"And here I thought that I was supposed to be the one turning into the blushing Socairan Lady," I said quietly, leaning into him.

"Storms save me," he muttered under his breath, but the corner of his lip tugged up.

"A blush *and* a smirk," I murmured. "Be still my beating heart."

Before I could think of something else to irritate him with, I was barraged with gasps on all sides from the villagers.

I sighed as they looked back and forth between me and Theo, giving us, or my hair, as I highly suspected, a wide berth while uttering the same Socairan phrases I'd heard Venla and other women at the castle say whenever I was near.

This is getting very old.

Theo ushered us forward toward the shop that Iiro and Inessa had entered.

As annoying as their reactions to my hair were, I couldn't help but look closely at those same villagers as we walked. They were a far cry from the people I'd seen at Theo's estate.

Many of them had dirt residue on their weathered hands and clothes. All of them were gaunt, with sunken eyes and sharp, jutting cheekbones.

My stomach twisted in pity.

The only place I had witnessed such malnutrition in Lochlann was in Hagail. It was rarely because they didn't have access to proper food, and mostly because they spent their money and time at the local taverns, trying to survive on ale or whiskey alone.

But here...here, all of them seemed to suffer, young and old alike.

"It would help if you didn't stare," Theo muttered under his breath, and I snapped my gaze to his.

With a slight tilt of his head, he nodded toward a crowd of onlookers. Their faces were coated in furious expressions as they glared at me. Not at my hair this time, but me.

I averted my gaze and looked at the shops and houses instead. Understandably, they were in a similar state as the people who lived here.

The buildings in the village appeared to have been well

built. It was easy to see that at one point they were even attractive, but time had not been kind to them. Many of the signs hung crooked on a single hook. The stone edifices were coated in grime, and many were missing bricks or had broken beams sticking out of the roofs.

This village was poor, and the people were suffering.

"What happened here?" As soon as I asked the question, the answer formed in the back of my mind.

"Our country depended on trade," was all Theo said in response before he opened the door to the shop and ushered me inside.

Of course they had.

All I could see was the angry expressions of the group of villagers, who clearly hated me for more than whatever superstitions they clung to. I was a walking reminder of my people who had cut off their food supplies, their trade routes, and livelihoods.

Stars, I would hate me in their situation, too.

CHAPTER 14

I nessa had done her best, along with the reluctant
help of the shopkeeper, to braid my hair and wrap it
in a knot at my nape, before tucking the few wild,
loose curls into the ornate hat.

The veil streaming down the sides and back did little
to conceal the mess of hair there, but Iiro had purchased
swaths of fabric for Inessa to alter the hats to accommodate my unruly and very un-Socairan locks.

I had never worn a hat a day in my life, and wearing
one now made me feel like one of the dolls my twin
younger sisters were always dressing up. I was certain I
looked ridiculous and was prepared to garner even more
attention when we left the shop, but instead, it was less.

Much to my relief, fewer people stared now that my
hair was concealed. It was easy to say I didn't mind their
scorn, but without Davin here to help me laugh at my situation, it was infinitely more daunting.

This time, when I wrapped my hand around Theo's
bicep, I didn't remark on his bulging muscles, but I did

give them a squeeze. He fought back a grin anyway, shaking his head like he was trying to rid himself of something as absurd as the urge to smile.

Instead of going back to the carriage, we continued down the road to a shop two doors down from the seamstress'.

I knew it was a bakery before we even reached the door. The smell of warm bread drifted toward me, making my mouth water. I practically purred when the baker offered us each a sample, waiting until I saw the others eat it before finally indulging myself.

The roll was soft and sweet and somehow didn't need any butter to perfect it.

My eyes fluttered closed as I finished the last bite, and when I opened them, it was to find Theo staring at me.

"What?"

He arched a brow as his brother and Inessa walked past us, back out onto the street.

"You are very expressive," he stated flatly, offering his arm again.

"Is that a terrible thing to be?"

His feature turned thoughtful as I took his arm.

"I suppose not," he allowed. "In the right circumstances, at least."

"Oh? And what circumstances might those be?" Both my face and my voice were just a touch too innocent, and Theo noticed.

Another blush crept up into his cheeks. I enjoyed it just as much as the first time, resisting the urge to let out a victorious cackle. It had really only taken me three days to break his stoic facade.

Though, why I cared so much was beyond me. In another week, it wouldn't matter either way. I supposed it was better than thinking about the Summit, though.

Theo cleared his throat, the perfect line of his jaw tightening and flexing in turn. "This is exactly the type of behavior that can't continue if you want to win the Summit over."

"Whatever could you mean? Honestly, Theo, your mind goes to the craziest places."

This time, he visibly fought to keep from blushing, and I let out an evil little chuckle. We continued walking in comfortable silence after that.

At least, it was comfortable for me. He looked even more uptight than usual, like he was forcing himself to be on his best behavior to make up for mine lacking.

We used up the rest of the waning sunlight by following Iiro into each of the small shops. Theo explained that it was always this way, anytime they stopped at a village when passing through, they purchased something from each store to help the commerce of the village.

The people seemed appreciative. They bowed low in thanks each time, muttering the same Socairan phrase that I finally understood meant 'thank you', words which were cut off entirely once they caught a glimpse of my hair.

It would probably do more harm than good if I chased after them and threw stray strands of my red curls at them like I wanted to. So, I rolled my eyes instead, convincing myself I wasn't fazed.

Theo looked back and forth between me and the villagers before escorting me around the corner, stepping in close.

"Here," he said, as deft fingers reached out to tuck the small strands that had escaped back into my hat.

I froze as his skin brushed against mine, from my forehead, down to my cheek and finally behind my ear. When I finally met his eye, I found that I couldn't look away from whatever was hiding in his gaze.

"Better?" My voice came out more breathless than I intended.

Theo cleared his throat, backing away.

"Passable," he said, and I noted that his voice didn't sound much steadier than mine.

"We have acquired your accommodations for the evening, My Lord." A guard approached, speaking the common tongue in his rough accent, effectively breaking whatever moment I had imagined just occurred.

I shook my head slightly, doing anything to think of something other than how stars-blasted attractive Theo's lips were.

He's my enemy. The man escorting me to my death trial. Even if that wasn't always easy to remember.

Movement stirred in the shadows behind Theo and the guard, drawing my eyes away from the two of them. A tall man in a dark, threadbare cloak was standing against the side of a rundown tavern, staring right at me.

There wasn't really revulsion in his gaze, like all the other villagers. Instead, it was something else.

Something far more sinister.

The glowing light of the lanterns highlighted the shadows of his face until he was close enough for me to see the large brand on his forehead.

I gasped at the raw, damaged skin with what looked

like a lowercase *B,* or the number six. His mouth opened wide, revealing rows of broken and decaying teeth as he grimaced at the sight of us.

Then he turned down the corner, disappearing from sight.

"Besklanovyy." Theo muttered the word like a curse, and I shot him a quizzical glance. He looked down at me with a grim expression. "Unclanned. We need to leave."

CHAPTER 15

We followed the guard down the dark road, with only the light from the lanterns to light our way. This time, I didn't link my arm in Theo's.

Maybe it was a good thing the Unclanned had shown up.

Teasing Lord Theo was only fun when *he* was the one caught off guard. Now, I felt uncomfortably conscious of our proximity. The fact that he hadn't insisted on taking my arm again made me think he felt the same way, which was a small comfort.

The guards stopped in front of a small house a few streets over from the bakery, opening the front door for us. We walked inside to find Iiro and Inessa already comfortable on the small sofa.

The house itself was very ordinary. There was one quaint room and a bed in a loft just above the kitchen area. A fire roared in the hearth, and Inessa sat next to her husband, quietly stitching a swath of the new fabric into another embroidered hat.

"Do you keep residences within all of the villages in your territory?" I asked.

Inessa glanced at me before turning to Iiro in a silent question. He pursed his lips and furrowed his brows in an answer that I didn't understand, and she turned back to her sewing.

"No." His tone was clipped. "Our only residence is the estate."

My expression softened.

"So you support the villagers by paying for use of their houses. We do the same."

In Lochlann, on odd occasions when we were in some of the outlying villages and needed to wait out a storm, we would either stay with a local family or they would offer to stay with a neighbor, but either way, they were paid handsomely.

It helped support the village financially, but also ensured that we were never too disconnected from our citizens to understand their needs.

Considering that Da' had spent a good portion of his childhood living in one of those small villages, it made sense that it was so important to him. I just wouldn't have expected it from Iiro, and I wondered if I had misjudged him.

Theo cleared his throat next to me, the awkward sound of covering up a faux pas. Iiro blinked irritably, then looked pointedly back at his brother.

"It is an honor for the people to host their duke," Theo

explained, his tone a little too patient. "They offer their residences freely."

I swallowed back my response. I hadn't misjudged him after all. He was exactly as high-handed and pompous as he appeared to be.

"You and Theo will stay next door," Iiro said, refusing to comment further on the other subject. "The guards will show you the way." He waved a hand dismissively.

What?

"Only Lord Theo and me?" I stared in disbelief. Such a thing was not appropriate, even in a more lax Lochlann.

And then, of course, there was whatever had happened on the road — the lightning between us when he tucked my hair behind my ear.

Of course. This won't be awkward at all.

Theo stiffened beside me, glaring at his brother, but said nothing to argue the subject.

"The two of you will find it quite accommodating." Iiro said, and I didn't miss the way the corner of his mouth twitched as he turned to face me. "Honestly, Princess Rowan. You're here because you're a criminal. We could hardly trust you to stay alone."

Theo once again broke in. "It's about your protection, as well. We are near the edge of our borders. It isn't as safe here." He sounded as if he were convincing himself as much as me.

Still, I was getting nowhere with this argument.

To give them a reaction is to give them power.

Be amicable and accommodating.

Gathering up what was left of my dignity, I turned back to Iiro and Inessa.

"Good night then, Duke, Duchess." I dipped my chin to each of them, then spun in the direction of the door without waiting for a response.

The guards outside escorted us to the next house over, which looked much the same as the one Iiro and Inessa were in.

I blew out a long breath.

Staying alone in a room with a man who was not family, no chaperone in sight. I could just add this to the long list of things my father would kill Theo for.

CHAPTER 16

S taying in a tiny house with Theo was exactly as awkward as I thought it would be. I took my turn in the privy, trying to forget that he was on the other side of the door.

When I emerged, my eyes went immediately to the single small bed.

"I'll sleep on the floor, near the fire," Theo said quickly, not looking at me.

I nodded because I sure as hell didn't want to sleep on the floor. Nor did I want to sleep in this stiff, uncomfortable dress. As terrible as the nightgowns here were, at least they didn't have stiff corset boning that dug into my ribcage.

This dress would probably suffocate me in my sleep.

Stars.

I wondered briefly if Sir Iiro was intentionally making my life as uncomfortable as possible, but it was more likely he had simply given the matter no thought at all. After all, it didn't directly affect him.

I sighed, poking my head outside. "Could one of you please ask Lady Inessa to come...assist me?" I tried to put it delicately.

They both turned to raise their eyebrows at me, and I suppressed an eye roll. Of course, they weren't going to listen to me. Before I could ask, Theo was at my back, barking something in Socairan.

One of the guards murmured what might have been an apology, taking off for the house next door. When he returned moments later, though, his expression was smug.

"The Duchess declines, stating that she has already dressed for bed."

I shut the door with more force than necessary, turning back to Theo.

"I'm going to need some help undoing my dress." I tried to speak without inflection, but even I heard the discomfort in my tone.

His eyes shot down to mine.

"Why are you taking your dress off?" he asked a little too loudly.

Fantastic. Now the guards would think I was putting on a show in here.

"I can't very well sleep in it."

"You can't very well sleep *out* of it when we're—both in here."

My fingers went to massage the bridge of my nose. "I'm sure Venla packed a nightgown in my trunk, and your brother was the one who insisted on her staying behind," I hissed.

Theo looked pointedly away, swallowing back what I assumed was another wave of aggravation.

"I told you, we are only allowed to bring forty people. And since you're a walking disaster who stands out like a literal flame, we needed every one of those men for our guard."

My lips parted in offense. "If you had given me back my sword, we could have done with one less. Then Venla would be here, unlacing my dress. But I didn't have a choice in coming here, in who we brought, in really anything since the stars-blasted tunnels closed in." I spread my hands out, a rare bit of frustration seeping into my tone. "What I do have a choice in is whether or not I sleep in this dress, and I have chosen not to."

His mouth opened like he was going to respond, but he clamped it shut again. "Fine," he snapped. "Turn around."

"Thank you," I said primly, spinning with a feigned casual air.

But there was nothing casual about a man undressing me, however reluctantly. I heard rather than saw him draw closer, a shuffling of fabric at my back that let me know he was moving nearer.

I tried to brace myself to have no reaction, but the moment his fingers brushed my neck, I knew I should have taken my chances with suffocation by corset.

It would have been better than the tension that thrummed between us, the heat that spread from every point of contact even as I silently ordered it not to.

Slowly, he untied the top of the ribbon. A shiver went down my spine, and he stilled.

"It's chilly in here," I lied. I was the furthest thing from cold.

"I'll add more kindling to the fire," he offered.

His voice was closer than I expected it to be, his breath caressing the top of my ear.

He seemed to be working very, very hard not to touch me, but it was impossible to loosen the ribbons without hooking a finger underneath them. My heartbeat was suddenly too loud in the silent room, thundering at a volume I was sure he could hear.

After a moment, I realized I didn't feel any motion. He was finished with my dress, but he didn't move, didn't speak. Once again, lightning crackled between us, the air vibrating with whatever had passed in this single span of time.

I reminded myself that he was escorting me to my possible demise, that he was Socairan and my enemy and a bit of a pompous arse clown to boot.

But my body didn't know those things. It didn't care.

Abruptly, he backed away, and the temperature dropped by several degrees in the wake of his presence.

"Will that suffice?" His voice was raw, his tone devoid of its usual condescension.

I nodded, not quite trusting my voice.

Theo went to add kindling to the fire while I tucked myself into bed, unstrapping my dagger and sheath from my thigh and tucking it under my pillow. Tension filled the room once more, but this time it was decidedly more awkward. I was the one to break it.

"How long until we reach the Summit?" I asked.

"No more than five days, if the weather holds," he answered, laying out his blanket on the floor. "Then they will deliberate for eight days."

He sounded relieved to be talking about something so innocuous, but I was doing math in my head.

I would turn eighteen that final day. A turning point in my life that I would reach hundreds of miles away from my family. Or possibly the day I died. Not wanting to dwell on that, I moved on.

"Have you been to one before?"

"Once," he answered. "They are uncommon. As I said, the clans exist independent of one another. Summits are only for the few things that concern all of us."

"Your brother said there were two other things that called for a Summit. What else could possibly concern all of you, aside from neighboring royalty illegally purchasing overpriced liquor?" I injected a healthy dose of sarcasm into my tone.

"Not much. Threats to the entire country, which really only come from your people. If the safety of any of the clan wives is violated, and if there's a blood debt owed between one clan and another."

"What if the safety of the clan husbands is violated?" I asked.

Theo barked out a quick laugh, quickly stifling it. "There are conflicts between the clans sometimes, but every man here is trained for the army. That's an expected casualty. It is the duty and honor of an entire clan to protect their duchess."

"Indeed."

Another reminder of why whatever traitorous feelings my body had were just those. It wasn't a bad thing to be protected or cherished, but I wasn't sure I would ever get used to not being *seen* or heard.

It was more clear by the hour that this was not a place for a girl from Lochlann.

CHAPTER 17

T he next morning was every bit as awkward as the night before, and I hadn't been able to resist mocking Theo for his adeptness at lacing up my corset. Of course, he had only given me his usual long-suffering expression instead of rising to my bait.

He then proceeded to be exceptionally stuffy the rest of the day, likely to make up for whatever odd moment we had the night before. Or perhaps he was only pouting because Iiro made him sit next to me, so Inessa didn't have to.

The woman was still either avoiding looking my way, or glaring at me intently as if it would fix whatever deficiencies I had.

Stars, I hope it works. It would make my life a lot easier.

My and Theo's legs kept bumping, our hands grazing, each moment more uncomfortable than the last, until the feeling of discomfort pervaded over the entire carriage.

My hands moved in fidgety patterns underneath Iiro's

watchful glare. I ignored him, stealing glances at the rocky landscape while only half listening to my lessons on how to act more Socairan.

Just as Theo began droning on about some aspect of Socairan female etiquette, that no doubt involved my simpering silence, I felt it.

It started as a tingling on the nape of my neck. A shift in the pressure of the air around us. That's when everything began to click into place, and I realized that the tense feeling I had been blaming on my interactions with Theo had a different cause.

A storm was coming.

A big one.

"When are we stopping for the night?" I interrupted Theo, trying to keep the panic from my tone.

"Am I boring you, Princess Rowan?" he sighed.

"Always," I couldn't help but shoot back, and Iiro glared at me.

Theo only pursed his lips, glancing out the window. "At least a few more hours, just before nightfall."

That was too long.

"I think I saw a storm on the horizon," I lied.

Iiro quirked a condescending eyebrow at me. "My guards mentioned no storm. We'll carry on as planned."

Heat flooded my veins, and tension filled my chest. The storm would hit before nightfall, but I had no way of telling them that.

If there was one thing that my mother had drilled into my head, it was the importance of keeping my fae blood a secret.

There were people who hunted us, even now, even

though all I had to show for it was an incredibly useless skill and subtle points to my ears. They would still want my blood, want to experiment on it, to see what I could do, or to force me to have their children.

So I tried again, a little more definitively. "I've always been fascinated by the weather. I've studied it extensively, and I'm quite sure there's a storm coming."

"And I'm quite sure a lifetime in Socair has given my guards significantly more knowledge on our weather patterns than the few days you've spent indoors here."

"Indeed." I forced an *accommodating* smile to my lips.

Perhaps this was the real reason women in Socair weren't allowed to go around armed. So they didn't stab the pompous Socairan men in their patronizing faces.

Still, I couldn't let it go.

This storm sent off warning bells all along my spine. It was going to be massive, and being trapped in it could be deadly. I had to do everything I could to make them hear me.

"It's only that, I was injured some years ago. I broke my—er—toe, and now it acts up before a storm." As soon as the words escaped my mouth, I wanted to take them back.

Really, Rowan, you couldn't have thought of anything better than that? Where was Davin when I needed him. He was a far better liar than I was. He would have found a way to make them take this seriously.

"Your toe?" Iiro narrowed his eyes like he knew I was fibbing but couldn't quite figure out why. Which was fair, since I most definitely was lying, just not about the storm.

"Yes." I was in this now. "My toe. I call it my weather

93

toe, and it's never wrong." I heard exactly how ridiculous I sounded.

Theo stared at me like I had grown a second head, and Inessa's gaze traveled to my foot in revulsion.

Iiro yanked the curtain over, looking pointedly at the clear blue skies. "Clearly, your predictive appendage has failed you this time." Sarcasm coated his tone.

"I know it sounds ridiculous—" I began.

"It sounds ridiculous because it is ridiculous!" Iiro all but shouted. Then, in a lower voice. "Amicable and accommodating, Princess. I wonder if you are capable of either. Not another word about the storm."

I clamped my lips shut, fury edging out the last of my embarrassment. Turning to Theo, I gave him a rare beseeching look. He might not be my ally, but he was the closest thing in a carriage with Inessa and Iiro.

He searched my face for a moment, long enough for the smallest bit of hope to bloom inside me. He surprised me by reaching out a hand and putting it on mine. A thrill went through me, even with the grim circumstances.

But that feeling fled as soon as he opened his mouth.

"I know you are concerned about the Summit," he began, in an uncharacteristically gentle manner. "But delaying it will not make it any easier."

I pulled my hand back. I couldn't entirely blame him, when the excuse I had come up with was a stars-blasted weather toe, but I knew he had seen that I was serious, had seen that I was concerned.

And he had brushed it away as fear when I had never shown him any.

I shook my head, muttering bitterly under my breath. "We'll be lucky to make it to the Summit at all."

CHAPTER 18

"Isn't it a lovely day?" Iiro had taken every opportunity since the mention of my weather toe to comment on the sunshine streaming in the carriage windows, and the light breeze dancing through the autumn trees.

Theo glanced between us, his disapproval clear, but said nothing, of course.

For my part, I didn't even bother glaring. The pressure of the storm was building, a tension I could feel as plainly as if someone were pressing their fingers along my spine. They would all know I was right soon enough, even if this was one time I wished I was wrong.

It was only fifteen more minutes before the warning cry went out.

Iiro sat up straighter, placing a hand on his wife's before leaning his head out the window. He called for one of the guards and there was a brief exchange in Socairan before Theo, Inessa, and Iiro looked back at me.

Iiro barked an order to the guards and the driver and

before I knew it, the carriage was flying down the road at a much faster pace.

My heart sank to the pit of my stomach, but I asked the question anyway.

"What's going on?"

"There is a storm coming in fast. We need to find shelter immediately." His tone was clipped and his expression furious, almost as if he blamed me somehow for making it come about.

I shook my head slowly, thinking of the farm we passed a few miles back. We could have sheltered there. We could have already been waiting this out.

A strong wind whipped in through the curtain, and the carriage lurched to the left. Theo's eyes went wide. He threw his arm out in front of me to keep me from flying into Inessa's lap, so I barreled into the solid muscle instead with a bruising impact.

There was no time to recover, though, as the carriage tilted to the other direction, sending my entire body careening into Theo's.

The howling wind quickly drowned out every other sound, and all I could think about was the fact that I should have fought harder to make them listen. I should have just left the carriage and ran for that house behind us, instead of staying here.

This is how I die? In a storm, of all the stars-blasted things?

Taking a deep breath, I tried to calm my frantic heart and think it through. The prickling feeling in my neck intensified, and the sky darkened so quickly it was no longer blue, but black as night.

And I knew, *I knew* we weren't in the worst of it yet. As

bad as it was now, the full might of the storm still hadn't fully arrived.

The carriage skittered off the road again, and suddenly, it wasn't the horses that were moving us. Several trunks came loose from the back of the carriage and went flying in the distance. Dresses and scarves, shifts and hats went soaring along with the wind as soon as they crashed to the ground.

One of the guards foolishly ran to grab them, only to be swept up in the same gale.

My hands shook, and a gasp escaped me as I watched the storm carry him high above the ground in a sea of scarves, twisting his body as if he were nothing more than one of the many colorful leaves floating along beside him.

I couldn't look away, even as he sailed back down to the earth with a sickening speed.

"There!" Theo shouted over the wind and my racing heart, pointing toward a farmhouse not far from us. "We can shelter there!"

Iiro looked in that direction and agreed, barking out an order to the driver, who was somehow still hanging on out there.

The harsh commands from the driver were barely audible over the chaos. There was only the angry howling of the wind, the sound of thunder rumbling so loudly, it reverberated in my veins and the cracks of lightning that made each of us flinch every time it struck.

I held my breath, and when I looked away from the window, I realized Theo was staring down at me with a look more intense than any I had seen him show before. When the carriage came to a grinding halt, I sprang into action, desperately clawing at the door closest to me in an effort to escape.

It wouldn't budge. My pulse picked up its furious rhythm as I threw all of my weight into the door again and again.

Iiro and Theo were having the same trouble with theirs until it wrenched open with a loud crack. My attention snapped to it just as it broke at the hinges and went sailing away, nearly taking along the footman who had opened it.

Giving up on my door, I scrambled closer to the other. Iiro pulled Inessa out of the swaying carriage before running into the house next to us. Theo stepped out next, holding out a hand for me.

Time slowed to a crawl, his movement stretching out over an interminable moment.

The wind howled and Theo anchored himself against the side of the carriage, still extending his hand to me. I braced myself against the wind, reaching out for him. My fingertips barely grazed Theo's before the carriage began to skid.

Theo's eyes were wide with terror as we found ourselves at the wind's mercy. He hung on to the outside while I was thrown back onto the bench behind me.

His pale blond hair whipped around and I saw his mouth move but couldn't understand the words leaving his lips. Suddenly, the carriage changed direction, and began spinning around and around, careening through the field like one of the wooden tops my sisters liked to play with.

My stomach flipped and my head spun at the dizzying speed as I was plastered against the inside of the carriage.

Theo called out and my gaze snagged on his before he was ripped away from the carriage.

The sound of wood splitting and crunching drowned out every other noise before there was a jolt that sent me flying backwards.

Everything was a blur until I was suddenly weightless for two impossible seconds. My body floated in the carriage before crashing down on the floor.

I braced myself for the next impact, but it never came. Though my body still felt like it was moving, the carriage stood still.

Scrambling, I shook away the dizziness and tried to climb out of the door. Theo had held on for so long, but the stars only knew where he was now.

A jolt of panic ran through me at the thought.

"Rowan."

My name floated toward me on a violent gale as I peeked my head out of the door.

"Rowan, let go."

I took a deep breath, something like relief flooding through me at the sight of Theo reaching his hand out for me.

"I've got you." Theo's voice was loud in my ears as he wrapped his hand around mine.

My head still spun, but I clung to him while we ran as fast as we could.

Debris flew past us, forcing us to duck or change course while Theo led us further into the field.

He came to a halt near a gray door built into the ground. The muscles in his arms strained with the effort to open it, but once it was cracked, he shouted at me to jump in.

There was no time to question him. No time to think. Another gust of wind made the decision for me, and I was falling into the darkness.

CHAPTER 19

The heavy hatch slammed overhead, but the muted sounds of the storm roaring outside still permeated the dank, frigid space.

It was so dark, I couldn't see my hand in front of my face, which was doing nothing for my balance. My body still thought it was floating through the air, the room spinning around me.

There was a curse and a scraping sound before a small lantern flared to life, illuminating the grim lines of Theo's face. It centered me, and I focused on him until I was some semblance of steady.

"Thank you...for saving me," I said, rubbing a hand over my very sore and stiff neck.

Theo was silent for several long moments. I looked up to find him shaking his head, pressing his sleeve to the small cut on his chin.

For all that we had just been through, it was nothing short of miraculous that we came away so unscathed.

"I wouldn't have had to save you if I believed your warning," Theo responded after a moment.

In spite of the words, he sounded more reproachful than apologetic.

"But?" I questioned him, dropping my hand to my side.

He cocked his head, tension hunching his shoulders. "But I wouldn't have hesitated to believe you if you didn't insist on being so ridiculous the rest of the time."

I bristled. "So it's my fault that I told you there was a storm coming and you didn't listen?"

"You told me you had a storms-blasted weather toe, Rowan!" He was closer to shouting than I had ever heard him. "Of course I wasn't going to believe you, and at least one man died today because of it."

His jaw tightened and he looked away. I wondered if he was more upset with me or himself.

"You knew I was serious," I said. I had done everything I could to convince him. "I saw it in your face."

"I didn't know what to think when you were making such outlandish claims. But life, death, laws, people, all of it is a joke to you. You make it impossible to take you seriously, then have the nerve to complain when no one does."

I opened my mouth to argue, then closed it again. Hadn't everyone in my life essentially taken turns telling me variations of the same thing? Both of my parents, and, hell, even Avani.

I love you, Row. But sometimes I feel like you're your own worst enemy.

I sighed. *Sometimes I feel that way, too, Avani.*

Whatever part of me had been offended effectively

dissipated with that memory, replaced by bone-deep fatigue. "You're right," I said quietly. "I'm sorry."

He huffed out a breath of air. "You could have died, Rowan."

It was the second time he had said my name. Just my name. No title, no pomp, no condescension. Just Rowan, breathed in a tone far more earnest than his usual high-handed manner.

I shook my head, trying for a teasing lilt. "That thought didn't seem to bother you much when I was in the dungeons."

"It's different now," he said.

"What's different?" I challenged.

"*You're* different." He clamped his mouth shut, like he hadn't meant to say that out loud. "You're just...not what I expected," he added quietly.

For a moment, there was no sound aside from the whipping wind outside and a clinking from the edges of the small space we were in. I could have asked him how I was different, but I knew as well as he did things had shifted between us these past two days.

And for once, I didn't want to needle at him. It wasn't a question he would want to answer. If I was being completely honest with myself, it wasn't a question I was sure I wanted to hear the answer to.

Not when everything was confusing enough as it was. Not when I might not live long enough for the answer to matter.

So instead, I made a show of looking around. "What even is this place?"

The tension in his shoulders eased, and I knew

changing the subject was the right move.

"Ironically enough, it's a smuggler's hole."

"How fitting." I huffed out a dry laugh.

"Indeed," Theo added with a nod of his head.

I sank to the ground, fighting back a shiver as I made contact with the freezing dirt. After a stilted silence, I spoke again. "So, if I... borrow one of these bottles, would that make a difference to my sentencing?"

There was a long pause, and I mentally chastised myself for making a joke when he had just gotten upset over that very thing. With a sigh, though, he responded.

"I suppose we would have to add theft to your list of crimes." He didn't sound precisely amused, but at least he wasn't angry anymore.

"Ah, but what is theft on top of the heinous crime of smuggling?" I asked.

The lantern light danced in his hazel eyes as he shook his head ruefully. He surprised me after a moment, though, pulling out one of the dusty glass cylinders.

"There. Now I've stolen it, and we'll never have to find out."

The corner of my mouth tugged upward as he popped the cork and took a swig before handing it to me. "My dear, Lord Theodore, what will people think?"

He scoffed and rested his head on the wall behind him, flinching when the bottles rattled as the wind howled.

"I didn't think you were the sort of person who cared about the opinions of others," he added after a moment.

I shrugged with more nonchalance than I felt. He was right. Usually I didn't care. *So why does everything feel different where Theo is involved?*

CHAPTER 20

You would think having to survive on Socairan vodka and little else for days in the tunnel would have made me sick of it, but I enjoyed the smooth taste as much as ever.

I especially appreciated the way it made this freezing smuggler's hole just a little less cold and how it numbed my sore body. I had never bruised easily, and any cuts I received had always healed relatively quickly. Rubbing my hands over my cold and aching arms, I could only hope that would be the case this time, too.

Judging by the pressure along my spine, the storm wouldn't let up any time soon. It would be at least a few hours before we could even risk the short trek to Iiro and Inessa in the farmhouse.

I took another swig, passing the bottle back to Theo. After polishing off a decent portion of the vodka, his expression was less guarded than usual. He looked at me with something like bewilderment. Maybe even wonder, though it was still edged with his usual exasperation.

"You are like no woman I have ever met." He tipped the bottle up, and I couldn't help but notice the way his lips pressed against the glass, and how his Adam's apple bobbed when he took a swallow.

Suddenly, my own mouth was dry. I reached out my hand for the bottle, my fingers brushing against his when he passed it to me.

"Or perhaps you have met many women like me. Only you aren't aware of them because you never let them speak." I raised my eyebrows in a challenge before taking another sip, smaller this time, since I didn't want it going to my head.

He shook his head. "Our women *do* speak. We just believe that women are to be protected and cherished, given the freedom to live their lives without having to worry about war and politics."

"Freedom isn't giving someone a small chunk of life and expecting them to be content with it," I said softly.

He looked thoughtful at that, then gave me a reluctant smile. "Regardless, I feel confident not one of them is like you."

"That's probably fair." I smirked. It was hard to imagine a proper Socairan woman drinking vodka from the bottle.

Then again, it isn't exactly appropriate behavior for a Lochlannian princess either.

"Is everyone in your family like you? Or are you and *Laird* Davin..." he smirked on his pronunciation of the word, then paused like he wasn't sure how to finish his question.

"The collective disgrace of the family?" I supplied for him.

He shrugged, nodding.

"I suppose it's a combination of the two." I found myself telling him, then, about my sisters and my cousins, stories of growing up at each other's castles. How I was closer to Avani since we were just over a year apart, but I still adored my younger siblings.

When I got to my parents, his features turned wistful.

"What about you?" I asked. "Has it always been just you and your brother?"

"Not always," he said. "But for as long as I can remember. A plague took my parents when I was just four years old. Iiro was only sixteen, a new duke with a floundering clan to run. He could have passed me off to a governess, but he insisted on raising me himself. He taught me everything, took me everywhere." Respect shone from his tone, and a deep affection I recognized well.

It raised Iiro several degrees in my eyes. He had his faults, but some of his behavior was more understandable, knowing how difficult it must have been to command authority at such a young age.

"So you're more like a son to him?"

"In some ways," he allowed. "Especially since he can't—never mind."

I shot him a curious look, but he only shook his head.

Silence fell, somewhat awkwardly, and I grasped around for something to say. His words from earlier came back to me, and I realized with a wave of remorse that I never even asked him about his men.

"I'm sorry about your guard," I said softly. "Was he a friend of yours?"

"Bogdan was a good man, an excellent soldier, and a loyal servant. He will be missed." His tone was controlled, matter-of-fact, even, but his jaw was clenched.

Then he turned to look at me, and it suddenly struck me how close we were. His face was only inches from mine, close enough for his breath to touch my cheek when he spoke.

"But it was wrong of me to blame you." He continued on. "The weather here has taken many lives, as suddenly as it can turn. And that, that is not your fault."

So soft, it was almost a whisper, he added, "But how did you know?"

I wished I didn't have to lie to him, that I could give him a truth as he had given me, but more than my own wellbeing was at stake if I revealed my family's biggest secret.

"I told you, I've always been fascinated by weather for some reason," I hedged. "You know when something just catches your attention and you can't explain it?"

He held my gaze for an interminable moment. "Yes. I know that feeling quite well." Then he shook his head and scooted away from me. "So your extensive princess education included weather classes. What else?"

In spite of the more formal tone that he donned, he looked genuinely interested. So I went on to tell him about how boring most of my education was, enjoying the scandal that crossed his face when I mentioned training with the soldiers every morning.

"And your father allowed that?" he asked, green eyes wide.

"Who do you think was doing the training?"

He actually chuckled at that, though it was tinged with disbelief. Then he told me about Iiro teaching him to use a sword, talking more than he had before. It was a far cry from the single sentences he usually bit out.

At some point, the noises of the storm faded into the background. It was easy to forget there was a world outside of this tiny space at all. There were no enemy kingdoms, no impending Summit, no devastating winds.

Just Theo and me.

I didn't hate that nearly as much as I should have.

CHAPTER 21

As the hours slipped by, the temperatures dropped, and talking began to take entirely too much energy.

We both knew the only way to get warm. It was only a matter of who would say it out loud first. Knowing Lord Theo and his overwhelming sense of propriety, I reluctantly opened my mouth.

"It's freezing." A shiver ripped through me, jolting through my already aching joints.

"We aren't in danger of freezing to death." He was back to his usual clipped tone, the one I was beginning to realize he used when he was uncomfortable.

Stars.

"I know that," I said in the overly patient voice I used with my youngest sibling. "But we are in danger of having one hell of a miserable night ahead of us." It wouldn't be warm until morning — not that I could tell him that — and there was no way the small flame of the lantern was going to be enough to keep me warm.

When he only stared ahead, I snorted, a white puff in the air in front of me. "Your scruples won't keep either of us warm, Lord Theo, and honestly. Don't tell me you haven't bundled up with your men before."

He nodded, once, a sharp dip of his head.

"Then how is this different?"

"You know how it's different."

"Do I?" I cocked an eyebrow, but the expression was chased away by another shiver. "Look, we can just put your cloak on the floor, and use my dress to cover us. We can stay mostly clothed," I bit out through chattering teeth.

I wasn't ashamed to admit that my practicality tended to outreach my arbitrary principles. I needed all the strength I could get to face whatever was ahead of me, and I wasn't going to have any if we spent the night half frozen instead of getting rest.

He watched me as another tremor overtook me, and finally relented. "Fine. Just...keep your hands to yourself."

I arched a brow. "You should be so lucky."

He ignored me, laying his cloak on the ground, then looked dubiously at my dress. I didn't give him a chance to change his mind, turning quickly and gesturing.

This time, when he undid my laces, it was with frigid, fumbling fingers. He turned his head while I shimmied out of my dress and onto his warm cloak, putting the full skirts to use covering me before he could catch sight of the dagger at my thigh.

He sidled in next to me, and I yanked his arm around me, having no desire to wait half a century for him to feel comfortable doing that when I was freezing. I buried my face into his chest, and whatever his original reservations, he pulled me tighter against him.

Within seconds, his body heat seared into my own, calming my shivers. A delightfully warm chill ran through me, and I pressed my frozen nose against his chest to thaw, too. Theo stiffened beneath me, but said nothing.

Even the roaring thunder and howling winds outside quieted while I was tucked into the cocoon of his arms, replaced entirely by the rushed rhythm of his beating heart.

I focused on that sound, allowing it to drown out every other thought until it eventually lulled me to sleep.

IT WAS WARMER WHEN I AWOKE. HOT EVEN, BUT NOT the unpleasant heat of the scorching sun, more like the intense, welcome warmth of a crackling fire on a wintry day.

The gentle tingling along my spine promised sunshine outside, but not enough to account for what I felt now.

As consciousness crept in, so did the startling aware-ness that the warmth was from another person. A large, muscular person who still had their arms wrapped firmly around me, their thumb making a slow circle on my lower back.

I opened my eyes, letting them travel upward until they met Theo's. He must have turned the lantern off the night before, but shafts of sunlight stole through the door on the ceiling, illuminating the golden sunbursts in his hazel eyes and painting the room in a hazy, ethereal glow.

My lips parted to make a joke, but something made me still my tongue. Maybe it was his searching expression, or the way he was wide awake but hadn't loosened his tight hold on me.

Maybe it was the way his gaze snagged on my mouth, his full lips parting in a mirror of mine. The way that every nerve ending on my body was suddenly intensely aware, trails of fire scorching a path everywhere my skin met his through the thin shift that managed to feel both like too much clothing and not enough.

He loosened his hold, his hand trailing from my shoulder down to my hip, his head leaning toward me just slow enough that it felt like a question, one I didn't know the answer to.

But I knew what I wanted in that moment.

I tilted my head up as he pressed forward, eliminating the space between us. In spite of the cold the night before, his lips were warm and gentle. A caress, a whisper of skin against mine that had a small gasp escaping me.

He made an answering sound low in his throat, angling us so he hovered over me, supported on each side by one muscled arm, but never breaking our kiss.

Some part of my brain was sending off alarm bells, telling me exactly how stupid this was. It was diligently listing every reason I should decidedly not be kissing Theodore Korhonan, a man who was bringing me to face my judgment and couldn't even decide if he liked me half the time.

But here in this dim room, cut off from the rest of the world, I couldn't quite bring myself to care. Besides, I had never been great at listening to that little voice in my head. That's how I wound up here to begin with.

I pulled back for a small second, unable to stop myself from taunting him. "Do you still want me to keep my hands to myself?" My words were a whisper against his lips.

"Shut up, Rowan," he whispered back, closing the distance between us once more.

His tongue teased at the seam of my mouth, and my body arched in response, my lips parting for him.

I had stolen kisses before, when I was supposed to be taking chaste, boring turns around the garden after dinner, but it had never been like this.

This felt somehow more real and less tangible, all at the same time. Like a mythical bird that might take flight at any moment, leaving you in doubt as to whether you ever really saw it at all.

I was so lost in the feeling of his body against mine, his lips against my lips, and the way my heart raced beneath my breast that I nearly missed the heavy thud over our heads.

We pulled apart just in time for a blinding shaft of sunlight to pour into the room, illuminating the vague outline of a large man.

"They're in here, Your Grace."

Indeed, we were. Half naked, flushed, and disheveled for the entire guard to see.

Just when I thought my time in Socair couldn't get any worse.

CHAPTER 22

My head was still spinning as Theo scurried toward the steps, blocking me from the soldier's view and ordering him away. The door shut once more.

"We need to get dressed." He stated the obvious, quickly putting on his pants and grabbing his undershirt and jacket.

"Mhmm," I mumbled in agreement, grabbing my dress.

I was suddenly very aware of how revealing my shift was and how much skin was visible on both of us.

The tension that hung between us was palpable. The mood from only moments ago was entirely gone now, like a bucket of ice water had been dumped on me while I was peacefully sleeping.

Theo did his best not to look at me as I slipped back into my dress until he had to come help me with the laces.

I was torn between wanting to step away out of embarrassment and wanting to lean back into his warmth, but he made that decision for me, putting as much distance between us as possible while he tied my laces with a perfunctory efficiency.

Clearly, he regretted the entire thing.

It was unexpectedly hurtful, even though I should have felt the same way. Especially now that we had been seen.

Once we were presentable, we walked up the small staircase back out into the open field.

The storm had been terrifying while we were in it, but it had done surprisingly little damage. I surveyed the fields, noting a few downed trees, but not much else, while I tried to ignore the judgmental looks from the guards around the ruined carriage.

Red threatened to creep up my neck and into my cheeks, but I forced it down. It wasn't as if Theo was getting any pointed looks. Of course not.

Stars.

Iiro and Inessa stood outside of a much smaller, simpler carriage. Wonderful. Theo and I could enjoy all the awkwardness of being squashed together on one of the narrow benches.

Squaring my shoulders, I headed toward the carriage.

Theo followed just behind me, muttering something sharply in Socairan, and the men averted their eyes.

"Good morning, Sir Iiro, Lady Inessa," I greeted, doing everything in my power to keep my voice even. "I am grateful you were both safe and that you found us."

Even I heard how ridiculous I sounded.

Thanks for finding me making out with your brother in nothing but my undergarments after a murderous storm nearly killed us all.

Inessa refused to make eye contact, which was just as

well, and Iiro only quirked a brow at his brother before we all clambered into the carriage. As I suspected, it was a family carriage, really only big enough to comfortably seat two adults and two children.

Even with my much shorter legs, Iiro's feet were in the space for mine and Theo's knee brushed against my leg.

Wonderful. My imminent demise at the hands of the Summit wasn't sounding too terrible just now.

Theo and his brother went back and forth in their language for several moments until they finally decided to speak the common tongue.

I could have given them the benefit of the doubt, since it was probably easier for them to speak in their native tongue when discussing such serious matters like their losses, and next steps and whatever else needed tending to before we continued on our journey.

But I had the distinct impression that most of it had to do with whatever did or did not happen in the smuggler's den. The furtive glances from Theo didn't help with that assumption.

Then Iiro said something that sounded distinctly suggestive, and Theo shot him a rare warning look. My cheeks reddened again, more from anger than embarrassment this time, but I said nothing.

The conversation stilled as Iiro called out for the driver to go.

"I am happy you were found safe." Iiro's bland tone was impossible to decipher.

I bit back a sardonic comment about how that was funny considering we were still headed toward the Summit, opting for politeness instead.

"Thank you." Rather than wait for another round of questions about my weather toe, I steered the conversation in another direction. "Did you sustain many losses?" My mind recalled the footman Bogdan flying through the air, and I regretted it instantly.

"Not as many as we could have, but more than we should have." His tone was flat, and he offered nothing further on the subject.

Time dragged more slowly after that, none of us doing much of anything to further the conversation. Every jolt of the carriage sent my backside jarring against the hard wooden bench, exacerbating the aches and bruises from the storm yesterday.

Theo did his best to maintain as much physical space between us as possible on the much smaller bench, but it was impossible. I couldn't so much as shift in my seat without my leg sliding against his.

Still, I had to wonder why he was trying so hard. Because he felt guilty for the things his people were obviously saying about me now? Or because he was ashamed of being found that way with someone from Lochlann, a criminal, *me*?

I told myself it didn't matter, even if my father's words were running on a loop in my head. *Can ye not go five minutes without doing something stupid?*

No, Da'. Apparently not.

CHAPTER 23

By the time we made it to the village we were staying in for the night, I was well and truly exhausted, both physically and mentally.

My mind ran on a continuous loop from wondering if Theo had felt the same things I did in that smuggler's den to telling myself I didn't care. Then it returned to the Summit, and I had to wonder if any of this mattered in the long run, anyway.

Once we reached the edge of the village, we pulled up to a farmhouse that was built into the side of a hill. One of the guards knocked on the door, saying something in Socairan before looking back toward us.

The man nodded and within a few moments, a family was exiting the house. The father bowed toward Iiro, who nodded in return, while the mother herded her two teenage sons and two small daughters toward their wagon, fatigue in every step.

An honor to house their duke, indeed.

Watching them niggled at something in the back of my mind, but before I could ponder that, the guards and footmen ushered us inside. They kept an eye on the horizon and their hands on their weapons.

"They seem more vigilant than usual tonight," I murmured on our way in.

"We're nearing the edge of Clan Elk's territory. Tomorrow, we will be on Viper lands." It was Iiro who answered, unsurprisingly. Theo had barely spoken all day.

A welcoming fire was already lit in the hearth of the cozy main room, and a half-empty pot of stew was simmering just above it. My mouth watered. We had a meal of hard bread and cheese with a variety of salted, dried meats earlier, but whatever was cooking there now smelled much better.

We sat at the rustic wooden table, as one of the footmen scavenged for bowls in the small kitchen and poured each of us a serving of the stew. The dishes in the sink were enough for me to see that we hadn't just stolen the family who lived here's dinner. *Though we were taking whatever was left over.*

That hardly seemed to matter to the duke and his family, though. They ate their meals, seemingly without a second thought. It was better than letting it go to waste, at least, so I took my helping, too.

"Aren't Viper your allies?" I picked up my line of questioning once everyone was settled in.

"They are," Iiro nodded. "but the Unclanned roam close to the borders."

I shuddered at the memory of the sinister man from the first village, focusing on my stew instead.

The scent of warm, salted potatoes with strips of tender beef and carrots wafted up from my bowl. There were also bits of onion, tomatoes and peppers in the thick, delicious-smelling broth.

"It is called *kavardak*." Theo finally spoke, still staring down at his bowl.

I nodded, though I wasn't sure if he saw me. "Shall I use the big spoon, then?" I tried for humor, and the corner of his mouth twitched in response before he went stoic again.

Of course.

I was scraping my bowl with some hard bread from the table when Iiro barked a few orders in Socairan to the guards. Theo's shoulders stiffened in response to whatever he had said, his knuckles going white around the handle of his spoon.

After a beat, Iiro turned to face the two of us.

If I hadn't known any better, I could have mistaken the look on his face for something akin to amusement.

But there was nothing funny about his next words. "Inessa and I will take one room, and the two of you will share again."

I nearly choked on my bread, though I should have seen this coming.

"Unless you would prefer a different guard sleeping in your room?" Iiro pressed.

Swallowing my bite, I forced a polite expression to my face.

"I'm hardly likely to escape when you have Davin at your estate and I have quite literally nowhere to go," I argued more calmly than I felt. "If you see the need for a guard, however, why not station one outside the door?"

I wasn't sure why I was pushing, except that the idea of being alone in a room with Theo after last night felt unspeakably awkward.

"Because then we would need two as there is also a window, and we are low on guards as it is," he said in the impatient tone of a man not accustomed to explaining himself. "What exactly is your objection to Theo staying in your room? Surely you aren't claiming propriety at this point?"

I sucked in an offended breath, but before I could respond, Iiro led Inessa into one of the rooms and shut the door behind them.

Clearing the annoyance from my throat, I shot Theo a questioning look, but his features remained stoic. "I know my brother has a pointed way of expressing himself, but it really isn't safe, Rowan."

When I didn't respond, he disappeared into the room that had been indicated. Instead of following him, I went directly to the privy, taking a moment to collect myself.

I had been unfazed before, when I was having fun getting a rise out of Theo. How had one kiss thrown me off so badly?

Sure, it was a really, really good kiss, but I wasn't this person. I wasn't this awkward girl who let a boy dictate how comfortable I felt in a room. Not even a boy with soft lips and chiseled abs...

Squaring my shoulders, I finished my time in the privy and decided that I would march into that room and not feel an ounce of discomfort.

I felt confident that I was capable of doing just that until I walked in on a shirtless Theo, the outline of his torso drawing my gaze like a beacon in the night.

Stars.

He froze, his half-folded tunic in his arms, still facing the wall.

"What happened this morning, can't happen again," he said in a decisive, cold tone.

I agreed, obviously.

So why does it feel like he just punched me in the face?

"Of course not." Did my voice sound as definitive as his had? "It was a mistake."

He met my eyes, the heat in them belying everything we both were saying. "Good."

"Good." I echoed. I shouldn't want to kiss him again. I shouldn't want anything to do with him. He was a never-ending cycle of hot and cold with no in between.

He swallowed hard, his eyes not leaving my face, as if he were reading something there that he shouldn't be. As if my thoughts were as evident as his.

Then he closed the distance between us in two quick strides, wrapping one hand around my waist and the other at the back of my neck. I stood up on my tiptoes, needing to soak in his warmth and closeness.

My life these days was like the storm had been, wild and unpredictable and endlessly destructive, but Theo was solid, steady, a mountain to shield me from my own hurri-cane winds.

He picked me up like he needed the proximity as much as I did, crushing me against him. Our lips crashed into each other's again and again in a desperate frenzy. What little resolve I had mustered evaporated.

Who was I kidding?

This may just be another in a long list of my mistakes, but stars help me, I would make it again and again.

CHAPTER 24

We kissed for hours, until the kisses turned languid and lazy and I could barely hold my eyes open. Then Theo softly kissed each of my eyelids.

"You should rest." He propped up on one elbow, and I pulled him back toward me.

"But this is so much more fun than resting." I spoke the words against his lips, and felt his mouth stretch into a smile.

"Indeed, but it won't be when my brother asks us why we're so tired tomorrow."

Well, that effectively doused whatever heat had been in this moment.

"Indeed," I echoed, backing away.

He chuckled softly, a deep, rumbling sound, then rolled off the bed. Part of me wanted to tell him it was stupid for him to sleep on the floor now, but I couldn't quite bring myself to.

Laying with him on the floor for warmth was one

thing. Even kissing felt relatively innocent, but I couldn't deny I was grateful he was chivalrous enough to sleep somewhere else.

Although, if I had thought it was awkward before asking him to untie my dress, it was excruciating now. I briefly debated whether I could just sleep in it, but I could hardly move my arms. Already, I felt suffocated.

I cleared my throat, forcing the blush from my cheeks, and once again asked for his help. He froze, but made his way over to diligently help me out of my dress, averting his eyes like a gentleman.

Then he returned to the fur blankets he had neatly lain on the floor.

"Goodnight, Rowan," he said softly.

"Goodnight, Theo."

SUNBEAMS STREAMED IN THROUGH THE WINDOW, AND I couldn't help but notice the way they danced across Theo's chest and glorious bicep where he slept on the floor.

I ran a finger across my lips, remembering the way his mouth felt against mine and how much I wanted it there again.

But that thinking was dangerous, because he might just wake up and freeze me out like he did yesterday. Soft snores interrupted that unhelpful line of thought.

Sitting up, I quietly removed my sheath and dagger from beneath my pillow, strapping them back to my thigh. Then I grabbed the pillow and threw it at Theo's perfect face.

He barely flinched.

One eye peeked open, and then the other, before a sleepy grin tugged at his mouth. "Good morning, Princess Rowan."

"You snore, Lord Theodore."

A low chuckle escaped him and he wrapped an arm around the pillow, tucking it underneath him before shaking his head. "I do not."

"In that case, we should all run for cover because I swore I could hear another thunderstorm rolling in."

"What, one that your weather toe didn't tell you about? I thought it was never wrong."

I grabbed another pillow to throw at him, and he placed his in front of his body like a shield. We were both laughing when the knock at the door sounded, bursting whatever bubble we had found ourselves in.

"We leave in ten."

The guard's voice, the reminder of what we were doing on the road, sobered me instantly. Theo lowered his pillow, his countenance more serious than it had been before.

He opened his mouth to speak. I was torn between desperately wanting him to say anything that explained what in the hell we were doing, and not wanting him to say anything that made this situation more complicated than it already was.

In the end, though, all he said was. "We should get going, then."

"Yes." I nodded my agreement. "Yes, we should."

CHAPTER 25

S everal hours slipped by while Iiro drilled every rule of etiquette he could think of into my head so I wasn't an embarrassment to him.

"Never address the dukes by anything other than Sir and their first name." At least that was the same in Lochlann. "And we do not curtsy in Socair."

"I should hope not. I'm lucky I can sit down in this dress." Today's ensemble was another stiff, multi-layered contraption that allowed little room for trivial things like movement or breathing.

Iiro glared, and Theo broke in, as he often did.

"Why don't we take a small break and give the princess time to digest this?" Theo's fingers grazed my elbow, and lightning zapped through my arm.

I appreciated his intervention, if only because I was exhausted from staying up too late the night before.

Iiro nodded irritably and scooted closer to Inessa, who was staring out the window and ignoring us as usual. Leaning my head against the side of the carriage, I followed her gaze to a group of boys around my age playing what looked like a version of Gorodki.

An older boy threw his head back and laughed, and one of the younger boys shoved him playfully.

Though they didn't resemble my family in the slightest, neither their features nor their clothing, something in the easy way they laughed and ribbed one another reminded me of home.

A memory came to me from just before Avani's wedding,

It was the middle of the summer, and we had taken a picnic to the lake. Gwyn and Gallagher were sparring while the rest of us egged them on.

"She's flagging, Gal!" Mac called. "Go for the win."

He sat against a trunk, Avani lounging with her back against his chest. She laughed, emerald eyes lighting up with mischief as she turned to face him. "Not a chance, Mac. She's faking it."

"Care to wager?" He waggled his eyebrows.

I pretended to gag. "The rest of us are still here, Mac, and you're going to offend Davin's delicate sensibilities."

"Ah yes," Mac cocked an eyebrow toward my cousin, who was laying with his eyes closed on the picnic blanket next to me. "Those delicate sensibilities must be the reason he's so tired today."

Davin groaned, throwing an arm over his face.

"I told you to drink Aunt Clara's tonic," I said.

"I'd rather die."

"You look like you might get your wish," Avani chimed in, laughing again. "What a legacy, Cousin. Death by hippocras."

Steel clanged against steel, and I looked over in time to see Gwyn holding two swords up in the air. "Victory!" she yelled merrily. Gallagher only shook his head ruefully at her competitive spirit.

"You know, everything is going to change after this," Davin sighed.

Avani shook her head. "Not this again, Dav."

"I'm just saying, you and Mac will be married and having little ones, and then Gwyn will be next."

Gwyn glared at him, and I winced. "Bold move when she has two swords in her hand," I stage whispered.

"I'll be Captain, you mean," she corrected, helping her twin to his feet.

Davin, in an uncharacteristic display of self-control, did not argue. He only shook his head. "Either way, change."

He was right, too. Everything had changed. Just not in a way any of us could have seen coming.

SOMETHING HAD BEEN BOTHERING ME, BUT IT WASN'T until we passed another village that I figured out what it was.

"Where are all the children?" I asked.

Everyone in the carriage tensed, and I got the distinct impression I had asked an uncomfortable question.

"One of the village *Babushkas* usually looks after the little ones," Theo finally said.

At my quizzical expression, he clarified. "One of the grandmothers."

"After all of them? She must be a very brave woman, indeed." I was joking, but Theo shifted in his seat, and Iiro's jaw went rigid.

"There aren't many. The Plague did not kill everyone who contracted it," Theo explained, hesitation clear in his voice. "Young children seemed to be particularly resistant to it, which is likely why I did not succumb to it. But those who had made the change toward adulthood...many of them were robbed of their ability to have children."

Iiro's hand went over Inessa's. She stared out the window like she was ignoring us, but her shoulders were hunched up around her ears, her features tight. A pang of sympathy went through me, but I knew she wouldn't appreciate that emotion coming from me, so I pushed it back down.

No wonder Iiro looked at Theo as a son. Did that mean Inessa did, as well? Was that why she had been even colder toward me today?

While I searched around for something to say, Iiro jumped in to change the subject somewhat forcefully.

"We are entering into Viper territory today, so we will be stopping for the night at Inessa's home estate, though her parents will have doubtlessly left for the Summit already as we were delayed. I expect you to be on your best behavior."

Well, if Iiro was unable to have children, at least he could console himself by treating me like one.

CHAPTER 26

A castle loomed in the distance. Green stones formed tall, imposing towers with spiraled golden domes on top. I darted a glance at Theo, and he nodded toward Inessa. She was excitedly sitting forward with a trace of a proper smile on her mouth.

As soon as we came to a stop, the footman ran around to open the door for Inessa and she practically flung herself into the arms of an older woman. They animatedly spoke back and forth while the rest of us exited the carriage.

The woman was clearly Inessa's relation. They had the same upturned nose and down-turned expression. And when they looked at me, it was with the same judgmental frown.

Lovely.

The older woman dipped her head in greeting to Iiro and Theo, before turning to show them to the door.

A gentle hand caressed my lower back, and I leaned into the touch. Though it was brief, the small reminder that Theo was there sent warm shivers through my center and reminded me that not everyone here hated me.

I took Theo's arm and pretended for all the world that there weren't bolts of lightning crackling under my skin at each point of contact. That I wasn't waiting for a moment alone with him again, where I could lose myself and forget about this entire stupid day and the several worse ones headed my way.

He escorted me through the long, austere halls of the Viper estate, each step reminiscent of Elk. Only this time, large snake statues lined the doorways, and massive stuffed versions of whatever reptilian monstrosities existed here in Socair were on display.

I cringed as we passed one with a head larger than my own, practically hiding behind Theo as we got closer to it.

"I didn't think you were scared of anything," he muttered under his breath.

I straightened my spine but still refused to look at the beast.

"Who said I was scared?" I asked incredulously. "I can be disgusted by something without being terrified of it." I looked away from the snake again, burying my face in his arm. "See, it's disgusting."

Theo's arm shook with his silent chuckle.

"Of course. How silly of me."

As soon as we got to the dining hall, Theo straightened up, his features going stoic again. Iiro gave him an approving nod, and we spent the rest of our meal putting on a show of distance for Inessa's extended family.

138

I DIDN'T PROTEST THIS TIME WHEN IIRO SENT THEO AND me to the same room. This house was vast and full of strangers whose motives I didn't know or trust, which led me to the uncomfortable realization that a part of me did trust Theo, at least with my safety.

Besides which, there was the obvious reason.

Sure enough, no sooner had we shut the door behind us than Theo scooped me up into his arms. I had just enough time to notice that my trunk was in the corner near a giant four-poster bed before he leaned down, closing the distance between us.

His lips were warm and soft, his kisses steady and gentle and everything I never knew I needed when the world around me seemed to be going to hell. I ran my hands through his short blond locks, greedily getting as much of him as I could.

"You should get some sleep tonight," he said when we came up for air, though he didn't sound like he actually wanted to. "You kept dozing off in the carriage today."

"I did not!" I protested, not entirely truthfully.

"You did." He backed away this time. "Shall I help you out of your dress."

"Why, Lord Theodore." I raised my eyebrows in mock scandal, though I knew he hadn't meant it that way.

Heat flooded his cheeks, but it wasn't all from embarrassment. I swallowed, turning around.

"I would appreciate your assistance, thank you," I said, straightening my shoulders and infusing my tone with mock sincerity.

I was expecting him to undo the laces with the same clinical precision as the first night. But this time, when he swept my mass of hair to the side, his fingers grazed slowly over my neck. Instead of going for my laces, he brought his mouth to my bare skin, skating along the line of my dress from my shoulder to the sensitive skin below my ear.

A gasp escaped my lips, and he chuckled in my ear, a sound that sent delicious shivers running down my spine. Suddenly, I was unsure again about us sharing a room like this.

I wasn't sure I trusted myself when the cold dread of the Summit crept into my body and Theo's lips were the warmest thing in this entire kingdom. I warred with myself for all of three seconds before a knock on the door sent us springing apart.

Theo opened it to reveal a middle-aged woman dressed in black, who was already staring between us with disapproval. Muttering something under her breath, she leveled a look at Theo.

"You leave. I help her change." Her accent was different than the ones I'd heard before, still thick with the guttural way of pronouncing their r's, but this one sounded slightly more melodic.

Theo nodded respectfully, practically fleeing the room. I was certain I was still flushed, my short, rapid breaths giving away exactly what had been taking place mere moments ago.

She didn't mention it, though, or speak at all as she helped me into another frilly, high-necked nightgown with a thousand layers of ruffles, this one in a pale lavender shade.

It was even worse than the last one. I was convinced of it.

When she finally left and Theo returned, the laugh he tried to cover with a cough confirmed my suspicion. He averted his eyes, taking a blanket from the bottom of the bed and spreading it on the floor.

Whatever part of me had wanted more of his perfect, distracting kisses had gone dormant with the donning of this monstrosity. Perhaps that was its purpose.

The Socairans knew how to ruin everything.

CHAPTER 27

T he next few days were a flurry of stolen kisses between long, awkward carriage rides.

Each time Theo's knee brushed against my thigh sent small sparks of fire through me. Whenever his hand happened to be resting on the bench between us, mine would find a reason to fix my skirts on that particular side, allowing my fingers to graze against his.

Iiro peered at us with suspicion, but if he commented, it was in Socairan.

Every night, Theo dutifully slept on the floor, and every morning, we went on about our day like nothing was happening.

Though, something was most definitely happening.

I glanced at his profile, the aquiline nose and the strong jaw, noting the pensive set to his mouth. *Is he thinking about the same things I am? That we were stupid for starting something we could never finish?*

It hardly bore thinking about, though. If the Summit voted against me, none of this would matter. Even if they decided to negotiate my return to Lochlann, that would be the end of this.

Theo was the sole heir of Clan Elk. His life was here, and mine never would be. Which was for the better, since the kingdom was sexist and its citizens took turns fearing and disdaining me.

The deep voice from one of the guards interrupted my thoughts as the carriage came to a halt.

There was a frustrated exchange between him and Iiro before we began moving backwards.

"What's going on?" I asked, as Theo stuck his head out of the carriage window.

When he sat back down, he spoke in the common tongue. "More storm damage. The road is completely blocked by debris."

A frustrated look crossed over Iiro's face, and he muttered something under his breath about Elk having superior roads. Inessa sighed, but didn't comment.

A few minutes later the carriage was turning, and then we were going straight once again. Whatever side road we had taken was decidedly less smooth, and the wagon wheels lurched and groaned, causing my stomach to flip uncomfortably.

I was so focused on my nausea and keeping down the stale bread and cheese we ate for lunch that it took me completely off guard when a sound of alarm rang out.

"Besklanovyy!" the guards shouted, sending panicked looks darting through the carriage.

There weren't many words in Socairan that I understood, but I remembered that one well.

The Unclanned.

A wave of shouts rolled down toward us from a hill towering above the road. We were surrounded by forty or fifty men, at least, all with the same branding on their foreheads as the man I had seen in that first village.

They ran with swords and axes and several other weapons that resembled farming tools, charging at the carriage and the guards surrounding us. There was no taking off to escape them, no running away.

They had us outnumbered and at a complete disadvantage.

I took a steadying breath, trying to run through every option we had, but there was nothing. All we could do was fight.

Theo and his brother spoke in rapid Socairan to each other and to the guards just outside the doors. My hand reflexively went to reach for the sword at my waist. But of course, it wasn't there.

I cursed under my breath.

The sound of steel clanging against steel echoed around us as the wagon came grinding to a stop. The guards tightened their circle around us, but it was clear they were outnumbered.

Iiro and Theo exchanged a tense, speculative look, the latter moving toward the door.

"No," Iiro said. "I'll go."

"But—" Theo interrupted.

"That's an order, Brother."

Theo clamped his mouth shut, but his eyes burned with fury.

Iiro squeezed Inessa's hand, still speaking to his

brother. "If it isn't turning in our favor, join only as a last resort."

Theo nodded as his brother leapt from the carriage.

The tension in the carriage was suffocating. Theo's knuckles were white around the pommel of his sword as he waited, respecting his brother's command. Several cries went out, and men on both sides fell, but Clan Elk was being pressed in on too many sides.

I could see it. Theo could see it.

Still, he waited, the burden of his duke's command weighing heavy on his shoulders.

Inessa grasped Theo's other hand, and he gripped hers back just as fiercely. It wasn't until several of the Unclanned broke through the defensive line that Theo abandoned the order to stay put.

With a quick glance at Inessa, he burst from the carriage door to fight them off.

I moved to follow him, but Theo slammed the door shut without looking behind him.

"Stay here, Rowan," he shouted, before diving straight into the melee.

I shook my head, my thoughts running wild. One person wouldn't be enough to turn this back around, but two...

If I had my sword, nothing would have stopped me from jumping into the fray. I cursed louder this time, furious that I hadn't fought harder to get it back.

But I wasn't naive enough to think that there was anything I could do without one. I would just be a liability. I knew it, and I hated it.

With all the grace of a dying frog, I lifted my heavy

skirts up as high as they would go, and grabbed the siren dagger at my thigh.

It wasn't enough to take on a man with a sword, but at least I wasn't completely unarmed in the carriage. If Inessa had an opinion about the weapon, she kept it to herself. Judging by her terrified expression and distant stare, though, I wasn't sure she had even noticed.

Rushing back to the window, I scanned the fighting men for Theo. My heartbeat thundered in my ears as I tracked him farther out onto the battlefield.

He had claimed that every man here was a soldier, and from what I could see, he wasn't wrong. Each of them, both those from Clan Elk and Unclanned alike, moved as if they were trained for war before they could walk.

Theo fell in beside his brother, and the two of them seamlessly protected one another with each proficient arc of their blades.

They took turns fighting on either side with practiced moves, raining down one powerful blow after another. Theo had said he could protect me, and I saw now that was true. But even he and Iiro could only fend off so many.

They were formidable, but the men attacking them were furious, their anger and passion fueling each blow.

Da' always said nothing was more dangerous than a man with nothing left to lose.

That's what these men fought like. It made sense, considering what Theo had told me about them, but it was still overwhelming in its intensity.

Inessa whimpered and scrambled into the corner of the carriage as one guard crashed into a door. Blood sprayed when his blade met the throat of the man in front of him, but not before the Unclanned ran his sword through the guard's stomach.

The men were surrounding the carriage, forming a wall to protect us. But that wall was weakening, little by little. If they failed, and we remained here, unarmed, then I didn't even want to imagine what would happen to us.

We were sitting ducks, just waiting for the Unclanned to overpower our only protection.

Inessa covered her mouth, ducking down low on the carriage floor to hide, her lips trembling.

Without another thought, I was already moving. I had respected Theo's order when I wasn't armed, or barely so, when I was no more than a liability to everyone here.

But fate had just hand-delivered me a sword.

CHAPTER 28

I untied my cloak and threw it over Inessa's back, whispering for her to stay low. Then, I used my dagger to make a long cut down the middle of my dress to allow for easier movement before slipping through the carriage door, closing it softly behind me.

Fortunately, the men were fighting in the other direction, so no one noticed me. I never thought I would be grateful for these ridiculous hats, but at least I didn't stand out like a bright red beacon in a sea of muted blonde and brunette heads.

I needed to keep it that way, at least on this side of the carriage. My presence would only distract Theo, and he would doubtlessly send me back inside.

I couldn't risk running around the carriage without a sword, though, so I crouched low, scrambling beneath it and crawling over to the dead men on the other side. Blood pooled on the ground, seeping into my skirts and staining my hands crimson.

I was no stranger to death. Da' had taught me to

protect myself, and it had come in handy through the years when the few straggler rebels or bands of thieves attacked us on the road.

Still, it was never a sight I was eager to see again.

Bracing myself against his body, I wrenched the sword from the guard's stomach. I was debating where to head first, when one of the Unclanned pushed past a few of the guards and headed straight for the carriage.

My heart picked up speed, and I took a calming breath, waiting for him to get close enough to take him by surprise.

When his fingers stretched out for the handle, I rolled out from beneath the carriage, gripping the hilt of my sword tightly in my right hand, and sliced right across his stomach.

His eyes widened with shock as he stared down at me, falling to his knees. I didn't wait to deal the killing blow. Within seconds, the sharp blade of my dagger swept along his throat, and his body fell to the side.

I used my torn skirts to wipe the blood away as my eyes scanned the fighting men around me long enough to assess the situation, peeking around the carriage to see that Theo and Iiro were both solidly holding their own.

A grunt of pain sounded nearby, and my attention snapped to the nearest guard. He was struggling with the Unclanned that had him surrounded and was one of the few men left on this side of the carriage, defending us as well as he could.

After a quick glance to be sure no one else was coming from the other side, and that Inessa was as safe as she could be, given the circumstances, I ran the few feet to his side. Using the advantage of my small frame, I ducked low and arced my sword across the back of the man's legs.

He cried out and fell to his knees, giving the guard the perfect opportunity to finish him. I turned to face one of the other attackers, but the man's face went white as a sheet. He muttered the all too familiar curse that Venla and the villagers had done each time they encountered my hair, and took off running in the opposite direction.

I didn't have time to think about the fact that I had lost my hat. Stars, maybe this put us at an advantage if I could scare away even a few of them with my terrifying mess of red curls.

"Behind you!" someone shouted in the common tongue.

I spun around, but not quickly enough.

Strong arms wrapped around my middle, hurtling me to the ground and knocking the air from my lungs as the brute landed on top of me.

Stars lined my vision, and fear pulsed through my veins. I couldn't breathe, but I needed to move, to fight. The man's full weight was on top of me, pinning my hands at awkward angles beneath him.

I knew I had only seconds to escape him. I blinked away the darkness and forced my arms and legs into action, shoving him with all of my strength. He didn't budge, slumping further onto me.

Just when I began to wonder if I was going to prove Theo right by dying on this makeshift battlefield after all, a guard appeared in my field of vision. He helped me roll the man off me, and only then did I see why my assailant had gone so still.

My dagger was embedded in his abdomen.

The guard grabbed it, reluctantly handing it back to me as several more of the Unclanned charged at us again. The sound of colliding steel and painful groans played on a loop as we fended off the last few attackers from getting too close to the carriage.

My breaths were ragged and my arms sore. It felt as if we had been fighting for hours, but the setting sun told a different story. No more than forty-five minutes could have passed.

The attackers started coming more slowly after that. Not many were willing to risk their lives for whatever they were after when it became clear that they were the ones outnumbered.

Finally, they stopped coming all together.

I scanned the field again, not able to relax until I caught sight of Theo once more. He was no longer fighting, but seeing to some of his wounded guards and discussing something with Iiro.

Once I knew he was safe, my body decided to completely give out. I leaned back against the carriage door with a thud, more tired than I had been in ages. Images of the battle flitted through my mind on an unending loop, always ending with one undeniable fact.

I took two lives today.

It was them or us, I reminded myself. In my mind, I repeated the words Da' had spoken when I came home after the first time I was attacked on the road. The first time I had to kill a man.

"Ye did what you had to and it's done, but dinna allow him to plague ye anymore." He lifted my chin with a calloused finger,

forcing me to meet his eye. "And never be ashamed of protecting those who need it most."

If those men had made it to the carriage and I hadn't had a weapon, stars only knew what would have happened to me and Inessa. I took a deep breath. When I exhaled, I pushed out any lingering guilt for the blood spilt.

"Rowan!" Theo's voice pulled me from my thoughts.

I looked around until I caught sight of him running towards me, his features slack with panic.

His chest was heaving, his face splattered in blood when he finally reached me, meeting my eyes.

"Rowan, what are you doing?" He gently took the sword from my hand, tossing it to the side. He reached for my dagger, too, but I held fast to it.

Theo ran his fingers up and down my body like he was searching for an injury.

"You were outnumbered," I answered his question.

He took a step back, his head tilting to the side as he studied my face.

"Crazy. Reckless. Girl." He breathed each word, his hands still on my arms. "Don't you understand that I almost lost you?"

His words sank into me, swallowed the air around me. For a moment, nothing else existed. No bodies on the ground. No men tending to the wounded. Just him and me and his words hanging in the air between us.

"Lost me?" I forced my lips up into a smirk that I knew wasn't reaching my eyes. "I wasn't aware that you had me."

He shook his head, leaning toward me. I should have turned around and walked away before his men saw us like this. *Again.*

We had no future, when I wouldn't stay here and he couldn't come to Lochlann. I wasn't even sure if I *had* a future.

And for all the time we had spent wrapped up in one another, we hadn't so much as had a conversation about whatever any of this was.

But death seemed to be following us around, waiting for its chance to snatch us away, and time felt so inevitably short. I couldn't deny that I wanted this, for however long it may last.

Besides, I never had been good at making the smart choice.

So I lifted my lips the rest of the distance to press against his. There was blood and death and the ominous weight of an impending storm in the air, but at least, for now, I didn't have to face it all alone.

CHAPTER 29

As soon as Iiro approached, Inessa burst from the carriage and ran into his arms. He held her firmly against his chest, his bloody hand running through her hair as he murmured things into her ear.

Watching them felt as if we were somehow intruding on an intimate moment. Frankly, it felt strange that Iiro had intimate moments, from the brusque exterior he had shown me.

Then again, there was clearly more to him than I had given him credit for. He had been willing to die in place of his brother, willing to die protecting his wife. Whatever his faults, he wasn't heartless.

When he lifted his eyes to meet mine, there was gratitude shining from his gaze, and something else, something that gave me pause.

Guilt.

Which made me wonder if for all Theo's assurances that the Summit would decide to let me live, that outcome was less likely than they would have liked me to believe.

Theo grasped my hand tighter, as though he sensed my sudden anxiety, and I let him pull me closer, let him ground me against the chaos that hadn't stopped assaulting me since the moment the tunnel caved in.

Iiro noted the exchange and shot Theo a questioning look. The one Theo returned was equal parts warning and pleading, and Iiro hesitated only a second before muttering something in Socairan that sounded like an order.

Theo gave a sharp nod in response. They both looked from the carriage to the road ahead, conversing in grim, speculative tones.

Before I knew it, Theo was lifting me bodily onto one of the enormous destriers — sidesaddle, of course — before climbing up behind me.

I was about to protest when he wrapped his arm firmly around my waist, pulling me against his chest.

"We need to get there quickly to avoid another skirmish," his deep voice intoned in my ear.

"What about the wounded, and the...dead?" I asked.

"The men will see to them. We need to get you and Inessa somewhere safe."

He spurred the horse into a run without waiting for a response, crushing me against his body.

The way he held me, it was like we were in the middle of another storm and I was about to be swept away from him. And it didn't matter that we were both filthy and smeared in other people's blood.

I sensed that this time, he needed the closeness as much as I did.

By the time we dismounted our horses in a clearing near where Theo said the Summit would be, I was stumbling with weariness.

The stars glowed in the sky around the crescent moon, enough for me to make out Theo's face when he looked down at me with concern. I started to lean into him, the way I had after our battle and the way I had on the horse, but he backed away, catching my arms before I fell forward.

I gave him a look that was equal parts confusion and irritation, and he shook his head, speaking in a low tone. "The other clans wouldn't like this. It was one thing in front of our men. Iiro can make sure they stay silent, but that isn't a risk we can take here. We have to be careful."

That made sense. It did. Still, there was a sinking feeling in my gut, like I wasn't quite standing on solid ground anymore. Or perhaps that was only my fatigue talking.

"I just want you to be safe," he whispered.

I nodded, grateful that someone in this stars-blasted place cared enough to look out for my safety. He wrapped his cloak around me in one solid motion, tucking my stray hairs under the hood before putting distance between us once again.

Then Theo and the duke spoke hastily in their harsh-sounding language, undoubtedly making plans for whatever the hell it was that we were supposed to do next.

"Our camp should be set up by now," Theo translated after a moment. "Iiro sent men ahead for that before we even left the estate. Tomorrow, we can see about getting clothes until the rest of the men arrive with our trunks."

I just gave him a tired nod. Theo's jaw tightened, and his eyes narrowed in concern.

"It will be fine, Rowan. I won't let them vote against you," he said quietly. "I promise, I'll protect you."

Something inside me warmed at that, even if it was chased out by a numb sort of fatigue. After all, what was another scrape with death after this past week?

Iiro gestured for us to follow him up the hill, pausing at the very top.

Moonlight glinted off pale canvas tents set up in a large circle, and the sound of laughter and drunken singing traveled up from around at least a dozen campfires. A river wound its way along the edge, and I could see the outlines of women doing the washing, even at this late hour.

"*This* is the Summit?" I couldn't help asking. "It looks more like a festival than a dangerous meeting of death and doom."

Theo shook his head. Where I expected to see a smile tempting the corner of his mouth, he was wholly serious instead.

"You can't let your guard down." He tried to smooth his expression. "And...maybe try a little harder to blend in."

Sure thing. That shouldn't be difficult at all.

CHAPTER 30

I iro led us through camp. Even at the late hour, the people wandered over to greet him and to question him on why he called the Summit.

His responses were a variation of the same thing, a return of their greetings and a promise that they would find out when everyone else did. He was more congenial than I had ever seen him, but Theo's body was taut with tension.

They kept me in the center of our small group, where it was easy for me to go unnoticed surrounded by their much larger guards, which was just as well. I wasn't ready to face anyone else yet.

All I wanted was a warm bed, or some approximation of that.

My knees weakened when I caught sight of a large navy flag with embroidered elk antlers in the middle. An enormous tent, easily big enough for ten people, stretched out before us.

Inside, there were three sections cordoned off by extra

fabric to create rooms just behind the main open space. I peeked through to find what looked like a makeshift privy in one of the side rooms. The other two held bedrolls, a double in one and two singles in the other.

I sighed, mentally preparing myself to ask Theo to help me with my dress where others could hear us, which was the only thing worse than having to ask him at all, when Inessa surprised me by approaching.

"I could help, if you would like." She had spoken so little in front of me, I was surprised to hear that her voice was light and chiming, like a bell, with the same melodic accent that the woman at the Viper estate had.

Her delicate features were softer when she didn't look angry or offended, and her large blue eyes were unsure.

"Thank you." I nodded.

She led us into the room with two bedrolls and gestured for me to turn around, then set to efficiently unlacing my corset.

"When you showed up," she said abruptly from her place at my back, "I didn't trust you. Your presence. Your motives. You were disrespectful and improper." She made a noise in the back of her throat, something between a scoff and a laugh. "You still are, for that matter. But today, that impropriety saved my life. I won't forget that. Neither will Iiro."

I was too stunned by her words to respond, but she wasn't finished. She continued speaking as her fingers went to the pins in my hair, gently removing them one by one. "I know my husband seems brusque, but he will fight for you against the other clans. Neither of us wants another war with Lochlann."

Grief seeped through her tone. I wondered if she had lost someone personally to that war, or perhaps the famine since, or both.

She walked away before I could respond, leaving me with the weight of everything our people had done to each other.

By the time Theo came in, I had taken advantage of the bowl of soapy water to clean up and shimmied into my bedroll before he could see me in only my shift. In spite of my crushing exhaustion, restlessness had my feet twitching and my body shifting irritably.

All I wanted was to reach out to Theo, to bury myself in his arms and let him chase away every thought from my head with his lips against mine. But he had stressed how important it was to keep our distance, so I did.

Theo climbed into his pallet, and we laid there for a few minutes, saying nothing, just listening to the faraway voices of the clansmen still catching up or telling stories.

Then there was a whisper of skin against fabric, and his hand nudged at the side of my covers, a silent question. Slowly I edged my hand out, placing it in his much larger, warmer one.

We still didn't speak. The only movement was his thumb running up and down my hand in a soothing pattern, until I finally drifted off to a fitful sleep.

CHAPTER 31

I woke up feeling more like myself again. Whatever melancholy had set in last night was chased away by the smells of freshly brewed coffee and meat roasting over a fire.

Nothing had really changed, after all. Iiro was determined to fight for me, Theo had said he would protect me, and I was fairly certain the Summit wouldn't actually risk a war with my people. More likely they would enjoy the power play of making me sweat, then leverage what they could from me.

Probably.

Theo's bedroll was empty already, but I heard the low murmur of voices in the main room. Wrapping one of the blankets around myself to cover my shift, I poked my head through the tent flap to find Theo and Inessa in the main room.

The latter was hastily stitching at a pile of fabric, but she looked up when she heard me stirring.

"Did our trunks come already?" I asked, though the

teal fabric she was working at was brighter than the fabrics Elk seemed to favor.

"No," she answered. "My mother sent clothes for me, and Clan Lynx sent a few things for our...visitor." She nodded toward a small trunk with a bright pink gown and a sunny yellow one.

Both colors looked dreadful on me, something I suspected Inessa realized since she didn't choose either to alter.

I looked sideways at Theo. "I thought they weren't our allies."

"They are staunchly neutral," Theo confirmed. "But it never hurts to ingratiate yourself to another clan. They know that as well as anyone."

"Which works in our favor," Iiro's voice preceded him into the tent, and the man himself followed. "Because it might garner you sympathy, the duke seeing you in his daughter's clothes."

I wasn't sure how to feel about that, so I only nodded.

Inessa finished stitching the hem on the fabric she was holding, then offered to help me dress for the day. It didn't take long to see that it wasn't only the color of the fabric that differed from the dresses I had been wearing.

This one was stitched more loosely, and the ribbon-style corset it came with was far less restrictive. I could even take a deep breath without wincing, although doing so certainly strained other parts of the dress.

Inessa shook her head. "I took the bust out, but apparently not enough."

She finished lacing me up in silence, and I took a

moment to admire the feel of the dress when she was finished.

It had layers like the others, the teal splitting in the middle to reveal a creamy underdress, and the skirts were still narrow enough that I wouldn't be running any time soon.

The sleeves fell past my wrists, but in loose folds, rather than the insect wing look from before, and though the neckline was high, it, too, was soft and unobtrusive. I let out a little sigh of relief.

Inessa made a noise that might have been disapproval, considering the style of her own dress was almost identical to the ones we had worn at Elk, but she didn't comment on it.

"They will probably figure out you are from Lochlann," she said in a low tone, fastening my hat into my hair and tucking my long plait behind the veil. "But we can avoid letting them know exactly *who* you are until Iiro announces it this afternoon. Besides, there's no need to incite a panic. At least your eyebrows are dark enough to pass for brown." There was the tiniest hint of amusement in her voice, and my lips parted in shock.

"Ah yes, wouldn't want to send any burly Socairans running for cover," I teased, and she shook her head.

Only when I was deemed presentable with each of my telltale strands tucked away beneath a teal-and-cream hat the exact shades of my gown did I emerge back into the main room.

Theo's eyes widened, and this time he let me see his admiration shining through. "Perhaps you will make a proper Socairan lady after all." He smirked.

I sighed dramatically. "I suppose there are worse things to be."

THEO LED ME OVER TO A COOKFIRE NEARBY, AND though he was showing me the way, my nose was the true leader in this situation.

The smell of bacon lured me with its smoky, delicious promises of a full and satisfied belly. Once we were seated on one of the logs surrounding the fire, a woman quickly filled two plates with eggs and bacon and bread rolls and brought them over to us.

Then the blessed creature left only to return with steaming mugs of coffee.

I was certain I had never loved anyone more.

I took a sip and surveyed the camp over my mug, noticing there were quite a few women here, more than would be accounted for by only the immediate families. I mentioned it to Theo.

"The clans don't get together for many other reasons, so they use this time to make arrangements, alliances. And most of them have bigger families than ours. My father was an only child, and my mother married into the clan from the royal family." He gave me a half smile. "Besides, as I said, we needed all the manpower we could get, escorting you."

I rolled my eyes. Though, whatever their rationale, I was grateful we had as many guards as we did when the Unclanned attacked.

My ravenous stomach growled and I focused my attention on my plate, feeding it one delicious bite after the next. Theo shook his head, a small grin hiding in the corner of his mouth, but he didn't comment. He appeared to be just as famished as I was.

Once my stomach allowed me to slow my pacing, I tried to do a better job of observing the scene around me. I hadn't missed the small glances shot in my direction or the whispered Socairan words that followed, but for the most part, the people nearby seemed only curious.

I wondered if that would change once they knew who I was.

Theo conversed with a few of the other men in friendly tones. I suspected he was going out of his way to take the pressure of their scrutiny off me, and to remind the other clans that they were on good terms, both of which I was grateful for.

Most of the men wore a variation of the coat and trousers Theo favored, though some were in brocaded tunics instead. The women were largely dressed like Inessa had been, or Venla, in the case of the servants.

When my plate was empty, the woman from before returned to take it away. Then she offered to refill my mug with coffee, confirming once again that she was my favorite person. I grinned and thanked her, sipping slowly on the brew.

Like Theo's, most of the conversations around me were in Socairan, and they blended into a steady hum in the air until a girl around my age sank onto the log beside me.

She was stunning, with large brown eyes and dark hair that fell in sleek waves around a face the same tan shade as Theo's. Her dress was similar to mine, only a coral color that would have clashed marvelously with my hair, and she wore a matching headband.

"I think that dress looks better on you," she said by way of greeting, her smile showing off a row of even white teeth.

"You're from Clan Lynx then? Thank you. It means a lot—" I began, but she waved a hand.

"It was nothing. I've more dresses than I know what to do with, and father always says I pack too much." Her accent was thicker than Theo's, and she had a lower, raspier tone than Inessa, but she spoke the common tongue fluently. "Besides, when I heard the *visitor* was my age, I couldn't bear the thought of you in those stuffy southern dresses. Though, I wouldn't have guessed the mysterious visitor was from Lochlann..." She raised her eyebrows, blatantly examining my features.

Instead of responding to that, I focused on something else she mentioned. "Are the fashions different in Lynx?"

She grinned in a way that said she knew that I was skirting around her comment, but was going to let me get away with it for now. "Things are more relaxed by the sea, as much as the other clans are scandalized by it. Though, I suspect I don't have to worry about being the talk of the Summit with you here." She laughed then.

The sound was soft, but the infectious nature reminded me of my sister. I found myself gravitating toward her in spite of Theo's warning to be on my guard.

"You're not wrong," I allowed, smiling in return.

"I'm Mila, by the way."

"I'm—" I stopped, realizing I wasn't supposed to reveal that.

Thankfully, Theo noticed my discomfort, breaking off his own conversation in Socairan to step in.

"You said you wanted to see the vendors?" His voice was that of a polite stranger's, rather than holding the warmth I had come to expect in the last two days.

I nodded with equal polite distance, determined to do my part as well.

"It was nice to meet you, Mila," I said, getting to my feet. "And thank you, again."

Theo whisked me away without waiting for a response.

CHAPTER 32

For nearly a week, I had been dreading the Summit, but now that we were here, it was hard to reconcile that this was the place I had been so scared to come to. That this was the place where I was supposed to be judged and very possibly sentenced to death.

It wasn't just the areas near Iiro's tents that seemed inviting. It was everywhere. In fact, it wasn't so different from the seasonal festivals back in Lochlann. There was music and laughter, food and games. It was nothing like the dreadful scene I had been expecting.

And I wasn't sure if that made it more or less terrifying.

What kind of people celebrated at the same events where they put people to death?

"Are we walking together...alone?" I gasped. "Such shame. Such scandal."

Theo looked skyward, heaving a sigh. "It won't look

any particular way. Every woman here is escorted by a man."

"Of course they are." Sarcasm edged my tone. "Who knows what we might do otherwise? Pick out our own scarves?"

He only shook his head. "It's for safety."

I couldn't help but notice he had reverted to the uptight lord I had first met at his estate. He kept a healthy bit of distance between us as we walked between the tents, listening to the thrum of conversation and laughter around us. Each section of tents was set up similarly to Elk's.

A large one was positioned in the middle, with several smaller tents surrounding it. There was always a cookfire off to the side and a post with the clan flag rising high above them all.

All along the makeshift streets were small carts filled with wares that each clan was known for. We passed a few selling jewelry, leather goods, small trinkets for luck, and impressively detailed tapestries, their sellers calling out in both languages.

"Why do some of you speak Socairan and others the common tongue?" I asked Theo, opting for a more innocuous topic of conversation.

He looked pleased by my question, and answered in the explanatory tone I had come to expect from him. "The common tongue is consistent, but Socairan dialects differ with the region. Some are similar, like ours and Viper's, but Clans Lynx and Ram are close to the sea. Their Socairan is so different from ours that it becomes easier to use the common tongue."

I nodded, thinking of the village accents back in

Lochlann. Though we all spoke the common tongue, some accents were harder to understand than others.

Theo opened his mouth to speak again, but my attention was pulled from his explanation by the sight of a small jewelry booth to my left.

It was laden with woven strands of silver and gold and an impressive collection of small, intricate charms. My eyes flitted from a diamond studded crescent moon to a tiny silver horse Avani would have loved, transfixed by the impossibly fine details on the charms.

There were so many, and they were all so varied. A ball of yarn with knitting needles stuck into it, a cooking spoon, even a bow and arrow.

Theo stopped talking then, watching me admire the craftsmanship of the jewelry. Each piece was another wonderful surprise. I'd seen wood carvings before, but nothing this small or this detailed.

Eventually, reluctantly, Theo pulled me away to explore more of the Summit.

The next set of booths made me wish I hadn't eaten my weight in bacon earlier. Well, they made me almost wish that, at least. Several of the vendors were preparing various foods at their carts.

I excitedly pointed at one of the carts with chocolate tarts and Theo laughed.

"Have I told you about our custom of pre-dessert?" I asked.

My mouth watered at the chocolate booth in particular, but I was desperate to sample from each of the carts. Several had small cakes and pies, while others had skewered meats, savory pastries, flame-broiled fruits and potatoes cooked in more ways than I realized were possible.

"Pre-dessert? No, but I have a feeling that whatever you say next will be riddled with falsehoods," he said, tilting his head to the side in a challenge.

I laughed and pushed his arm before wrapping mine around it.

"Theo—"

He abruptly cleared his throat, and took a step away. "Such informality, Princess Rowan," he said, red creeping up into his cheeks as his eyes darted around the crowd.

I opened my mouth to retort, but closed it again when I saw that people were watching us closely with shocked expressions.

Seriously?

"My apologies, Lord Theodore," I said, pulling my hand away and dipping my head in a respectful nod. "I must have been overtaken by the excitement of the Summit."

The latter part I added in a drier tone.

Theo relaxed a little at that before lowering his voice.

"If we buy you *pre-dessert*, as you call it, will you promise to behave then?"

I made a show of thinking it over before shrugging one shoulder.

"Pre-dessert will probably buy my good behavior for at least a quarter of an hour." I rushed toward one of the booths, resisting the urge to grab his wrist and tug him along.

"Don't worry," Theo chuckled, coming up beside me. "They will not likely run out."

Rather than lend reassurance, something about his words bothered me, but it took me a moment to figure out what it was. I stopped walking, turning to look up at him.

"But, in the villages..." I couldn't help but contrast this surplus with the thin, jutting bones on the seller and in the villages we had passed through.

"Ah," he said, understanding creeping into his tone. "Some fare better than others, but these sellers will see more coin from this Summit than they will in months peddling on the roads or manning their shops, and that money will feed back into their villages."

That made sense. Maybe that was why everyone here seemed happier, more relaxed than they had on the roads. They knew they would have the means to feed their families in the months to come.

"I'm surprised, though," I mused, reflecting on that. "I thought the clans would be more...combative."

We continued walking toward the chocolate booth, where I was even happier to spend my coin now. Or Theo's coin, as the case may be.

"Oh, they are." He chuckled. "But even if we are warring in the world outside, there's a truce here enforced by each Clan Duke. Any blood that is spilled without the consensus of the clan leaders is punishable by death or being removed from your clan."

"Any blood? Even if it was an accident?" I asked in a lighter tone, arching an eyebrow.

"All blood." He gave me a pointed look. "Is there something you're planning that I should know about?"

"I would just like to know all of my options should I

unwittingly be responsible for someone's demise," I said, arching a brow.

Theo laughed.

"Of course you would. I can see it now, you telling someone about your weather-toe and them falling back into a fire from pure shock." He shook his head. "And this is why there is death *or* clan loss. Death is for the *accidental* murders. Losing your clan is for when it is intentional."

"Well," I considered aloud, "I don't have a clan, so I guess if I murder someone, I should make it intentional."

Theo looked like he didn't quite know how to respond to that, settling for a startled laugh that he quickly smothered.

"Why don't we get that pre-dessert you mentioned, then, lest you intentionally murder me?" He wasn't quite smiling, but his shoulders had relaxed once more.

Between that and the chocolate, I considered the morning a win.

CHAPTER 33

We were nearing Clan Elk's tent when the raucous noise of booing and cheers reached our ears. I stopped cautiously, but Theo showed no signs of alarm.

He shook his head at my expression and ran a hand over the back of his neck.

"It's only the brawls." There was a slight longing to his tone.

"The brawls?" I raised an eyebrow.

"Yes, but they're silly, really." He shrugged with more sheepishness than I had seen in him. "Men from different clans compete in fighting."

Several of the people around us headed in the direction of the cacophony, all of them speaking animatedly about which clans they hoped would compete.

"Do you want to join the competition?"

"No, of course not." He shook his head. "I'm escorting you." But a fresh round of cheers went up, and his eyes drifted toward the sound.

A small laugh escaped me. This was almost better than seeing him blush. "I could use a nap anyway. Why don't you go, and I'll meet you back at the tent?"

"Are you sure?" he asked, his hazel eyes lighting up with excitement.

I nodded. "Of course."

He hesitated, clearly still debating what to do.

We eventually compromised when I allowed him to walk me back to Elk's tent. I waved goodbye before passing the four guards standing at the entrance, nodding to them as I entered.

I hadn't been inside the tent for more than a handful of minutes before I promptly spun around and exited again.

A tiny twinge of guilt pricked at my conscience, but...I hadn't technically lied. In fairness, I *could* have used a nap. I just wasn't going to take one.

And I *would* meet him back at the tent once I was done watching.

The sound of booing reached me from the direction of the fights, and I chewed thoughtfully on the inside of my cheek. I had seen a small dose of Theo in action when we had gotten attacked, but the focus then had been staying alive. I was curious to see his training up close.

So, I strode confidently out into the direction of the brawls.

The two roaring crowds on either side of a makeshift arena made it easy enough to find. My presence garnered more than a few looks, but no one actively tried to stop me as I squeezed my way toward the front so I could see.

I was halfway through the large, sweaty crowd when a

man yelled something in the common tongue. I didn't catch much, but "Theodore" rang out loud and clear.

I pushed my way forward with a little more urgency. There was no way I would catch any of it standing behind men a foot taller than me. Finally, I managed to get somewhere close to the actual ring.

Theo and another man stood across from one another, shirtless.

It was a sight to behold, all tan, defined abs and bulky biceps.

In a flurry of movement, they flew at one another, narrowly dodging the other's fist. Theo gave nothing away as he waited for the smaller man to attack once again. As soon as the man did, Theo went low and swept his legs out from underneath him, knocking him to the ground.

Cheers rang out, and a few boos as well.

Theo backed up, a large smile taking over his face as he waited for his opponent to rise. When the man was back on steady feet, he said something to Theo in Socairan that made everyone laugh, including Theo.

Then the man was flying at him again.

Where Theo used targeted, powerful blows, the shorter man was all fast moves and quick, relentless hits. I winced when his fist made impact with Theo's side several times in a row. Theo grimaced, backing away, even though he had a wide opening when the man swung too hard and missed.

Again and again, they pummeled each other with practiced skill.

I was staring at them, transfixed, when a voice to my

right startled me. "My coin is on Tuomo. He's smaller, but he's fast."

The voice was deep with almost no trace of an accent, but I didn't tear my eyes from Theo long enough to put a face to it.

"No," I argued. "Tuomo is wearing himself out too fast with those unrelenting strikes. Theo—dore," I hastily tacked on the end of his name before I was caught being *informal* again, "is saving his energy. He'll come in with the heavy blows soon and end this."

Sure enough, a few minutes passed and Tuomo's movements got slower. Theo came in with a solid right punch, followed quickly by one from the left. The smaller man went down.

I turned to the man at my right with a victorious smirk I couldn't quite suppress. He stood closer to me than I realized, enough that I could make out the intricate black-on-black stitching of his finely made tunic.

My gaze traveled upward to his bemused smile, only to watch it morph into something more sinister when his gray eyes landed on mine. I tried to step backward, but there were people crowding behind me.

"Who are you?" the man demanded. His gaze shot to my hat, and he narrowed his eyes as though he could see right through it.

"Who are you?" I shot back, already failing in acting like a demure lady.

Oh well. The man in front of me couldn't have been much older than I was. It wasn't like he would be on the Summit, though I supposed he could still run tattling.

"I'm—"

"Lord Evander," Theo's voice startled me from my left, louder than I expected it to be now that the noise of the fight had died down.

He must have jumped over the double-log barrier to get here so quickly. For all that we were supposed to be hiding what was between us, he hooked an arm around me and pulled me against him, away from the other Lord.

"Did you need something?" Theo's voice was cold and commanding.

Evander... The name pulled at my memory, and I tried to remember what Iiro had mentioned about him. Just that he was from Bear, and worse than his father.

Clearly, there was no love lost between him and Theo, judging by the tension rippling off them both. Lord Evander's stormy gray eyes never left mine, though, twin orbs of disdain.

"I asked you who you were." His high-handed tone was even worse than Iiro's.

I lifted my chin. "Ah, but you didn't ask nicely."

He narrowed his eyes, an expression I couldn't read crossing his face. Before he could respond, Theo steered us away, making for the outside of the circle.

The crowd parted for him, either because they had just seen him in action or just because he was a man, and I resisted the urge to scowl. I wasn't the only one. Aggravation emanated off Theo in waves.

Only when we were all the way in our tent did he finally come to a halt, spinning me toward him.

"What were you doing over there? Do you realize the kind of danger you're in from the other clans? Especially from Bear?" He added the last part a little quieter, his eyes softening as he looked at me.

"To be fair, I did only promise you fifteen minutes of good behavior. So, really, this is on you." I gave him a wry grin, one that he fought not to return.

He squeezed his eyes shut, and I got the sense he was slowly counting backward from ten.

"You said there was a truce," I reminded him.

"Between the clans, of which you are not. And even then, that's not to say no one ever breaks it and risks the consequences." He sighed, massaging the bridge of his nose between his thumb and forefinger. "I swear, Rowan. One way or another, you are determined to get yourself killed."

CHAPTER 34

He left me to consider that thought while he went to *attend* to a few things, not even bothering to stay and clean up after his brawl.

Before he left, he pleaded for me to remain in the tent. Then, for good measure, he stopped to talk to the guards on the way out, most likely to tell them not to let me leave.

Usually, that would have rankled me, but this time, it was fair. Even if the guards weren't there, I had already decided to respect his wishes and stay put. And really, it was the least I could do, knowing he was essentially my keeper while we were here, and I was apparently making his job very difficult.

Plus, I found that I no longer liked when he was upset with me.

I paced the empty tent, avoiding the thoughts that kept trying to creep in through the quiet. Ones about what the Summit meeting would look like, how Davin was faring back at Theo's estate, how my family was dealing with the news of our disappearance.

Shaking my head, I stamped that last thought out for good.

No good could come from dwelling on what I couldn't change.

I filled the rest of my time looking through the gowns that Lady Mila had sent over, and silently thanking her for providing options that weren't as rigid as the ones from Clan Elk.

When Theo finally returned, I took a grateful breath that I no longer had to suffer with myself as my only company.

I was fully prepared for more tension to descend upon the already overly-burdened tent of awkwardness, but instead, he had a shy smile on his face, all traces of earlier annoyance having vanished.

He came straight to me, holding out a bracelet of woven silver and gold twisted over each other.

"I seem to recall you saying something about friendship bracelets?" Mirth sparkled in his eyes, but it took me a moment to place the reference.

When I did, I threw my head back and laughed. It had been shortly after he brought Davin and me up from the dungeons, when he removed our rope bindings. "I can't believe you remember that."

"You're not easy to forget."

Warmth unfurled inside of me with an intensity that was rather terrifying. Between this and all of the moments we shared on the road, it was too easy to forget who Theo and I were supposed to be and why we were here.

Clearing my throat, I took a step back.

"Why, thank you, Lord Theo."

"Of course." He inclined his head. "May I?"

I held my arm out in the space between us, and Theo went to gently clasp the bracelet around my wrist. His fingers brushed the delicate skin there, and tendrils of heat crept from the pinpoints of contact.

I pulled my wrist back only to see something I hadn't noticed before. One of the charms from the booth we had visited, a detailed silver carving of the most beautiful flower I had ever seen. I gasped, meeting Theo's eyes.

"It's a Lotus flower. They're rare, complex flowers. Difficult to keep alive." The corner of his mouth tilted, and it took everything I had not to lean forward on my toes and press my lips against that smirk.

"That doesn't sound like anyone I know," I said instead. Then, in a more serious tone, "Thank you. Sincerely."

He looked away. "Well, you could hardly be a proper Socairan woman without one." At my questioning glance, he expounded. "Most women don't leave home without them. Even the villagers have a version of them, though they are usually leather bands and trinkets carved from wood. They get hidden under the long sleeves in Autumn, but in the Summer you'll be able to show..." He trailed off, and I wondered if he realized what he had just let slip.

The idea of me still being here in the Summer had never been raised. Either the Summit would vote against me, and I wouldn't be anywhere, or they would let me go home, and Summer was well after the pass opened.

But Theo had spoken about it like he expected me to be here then, or at least like he wanted me to be...

The idea sent a thrum of...something through me, that might have been terror or elation or any of a thousand emotions in between. Whatever it was, I didn't have words for it.

So I gave into my earlier impulse, standing on my tiptoes and leaning forward hesitantly to press my mouth against his. I had only closed half the distance when he leaned down, wrapping his arms around me and kissing me with what I might have called desperation on another person.

"We'll get through this," he murmured against my lips. "One way or another."

ON THE TOUR EARLIER, I HAD SOMEHOW MISSED THE ominous black tent in the very center of the encampment. That, or Theo had intentionally kept me away from it.

Torches lit the path leading up to the entrance, while nine heavily armed guards blocked anyone from entering, each of them wearing a color to represent the clan they were from. All of them faced forward with the same serious expression, as if they were an army preparing for an approaching enemy.

And maybe they were.

I took a deep breath, straightening my spine, and put one foot in front of the other to keep moving forward.

Because that's what you do when you're headed toward certain death, right? You go to it willingly, like a naive pig to the slaughter.

There had been times this past week when I let myself forget what this was all about, forget that I was a prisoner at all. Standing before this tent, it was impossible to ignore.

At least Davin had stayed behind, relatively safe. *Though, I could have used his commentary to lighten the mood right about now...*

Theo stopped walking, his body shifting to face me.

"Remember, we need them on our side." His fists clenched at his sides, and his brows were pinched with worry. "Don't speak up unless you are asked a direct question, and just—" His voice trailed off. "We will do our best to protect you, but they need to see you as one of their own."

There was something in his eyes that made me want to believe that there was a way out of this. He seemed so sure, so confident, that for a moment I did believe him.

That belief died the moment we entered the tent.

The space was fraught with tension. It thrummed in the air and through each and every one of the men at the table. Remembering Iiro's instructions, I gave a demure nod to each of them in turn, taking advantage of the eye contact to scrutinize their features for signs of how they might lean on this issue.

The expressions were largely closed off, but not openly hostile. I had almost begun to relax when my gaze landed on the occupant of the seventh chair.

My heart dropped like a stone into my stomach, and a small noise of disbelief escaped me.

ROBIN D. MAHLE & ELLE MADISON

What is he doing here?

Haughty gray eyes stared back at me, an amused smirk mocking my surprise. It was the young lord I had run into scarcely an hour ago, the one who already seemed to suspect who I was. And hated me for it.

Lord Evander's expression turned to open disdain when I stepped into the light. I swallowed hard, unease quickening my pulse.

Less than a day in, and there was already one vote against me.

CHAPTER 35

"Der'mo." Theo muttered the word under his breath.

I didn't need to speak Socairan to gather the general meaning.

Taking a breath, he straightened his shoulders and put on his usual stoic expression. He led me to one side of the semi-circle shaped table, gesturing for me to sit at an empty chair facing the clan leaders and the few lords who sat behind them. Their heirs, I assumed, from the way Theo joined them.

A chill ran through me as soon as he left my side.

Forcing my features into a calm neutrality, I did my best to present the portrait of Socairan contrition, even though I felt like the complete opposite.

The clan lords narrowed their eyes, first at me and then Iiro in suspicion, but the duke didn't seem to mind the scrutiny at all. His posture was relaxed, his expression confident, and when he spoke, his voice commanded the attention of the room.

He addressed the leaders in the common tongue, a dry recounting of sending his brother out on patrols only to wind up with a most unusual prisoner.

Several sets of wary eyes snapped to me.

"You may remove your hat now," Iiro ordered.

"Gird your loins, gentlemen," I mumbled under my breath, struggling with the well-placed pins that Inessa had used to keep my curls at bay.

Judging by the way Iiro stared daggers at me and Theo just shook his head, I hadn't been as quiet as I meant to be. Fortunately, my hair took the scrutiny off my words.

I had barely slid the hat from my head when gasps sounded throughout the room, one of the dukes going so far as to physically recoil from my hair. I bit back a sigh.

His loins had not, in fact, been girded.

The other faces were a mix of shock, disgust and disbelief. Everyone's but Lord Evander's, that is. He stared at me through narrowed eyes and a carefully guarded expression that gave no hint to his feelings.

"This proves nothing," the man next to Iiro declared loudly.

His words were heavily accented, but in a different way than I'd heard before, almost as if he were trying to swallow his vowels. "There are many fire-heads in the Loch Lands."

He pounded his fist on the table, and someone further down chimed in to agree.

"What are you getting at, Iiro? As Bison said, she could be anyone," questioned a man with a long gray beard in a red tunic.

A few others went back and forth in a blend of

Socairan and the common tongue, making me dizzy with all of the noise.

Iiro held up a hand to quiet the room, and the arguments died down, some far more reluctantly than others.

"Your ring, please." He held out an imperious hand.

My hand immediately shot to the chain around my neck that I never took off. Untucking it from the front of my dress, I pulled the chain around my hair and stood to hand it to Iiro.

Obviously, this was important for my case, but that ring was one of the only pieces of home I had with me.

At least I still had my dagger.

He passed my signet ring around the table, allowing the men to see the sword and shield of Lochlann, a symbol they knew, and then pointed to my tree in the middle.

"As you can see. It is a rowan tree, for their Rowan child."

I choked on a laugh. Who knew Iiro had such a flair for theatrics?

"Named after her grandfather, King Rowan of Luan," he continued on.

Ah yes, my namesake. The revered king, the strong and steady leader.

If only he could see me now.

The poor man probably rolled over in his grave when *I* was the one named after him instead of my sister.

Someone to my left cleared his throat, drawing the room's attention.

Lord Evander.

The arrogant man sat back in his chair, the very picture of confidence and control as he spoke.

"And how do we know that this ring isn't a farce? You could have had it made. Why do you expect us to believe you?"

Iiro looked down his nose at the much younger lord, hesitating before he replied.

"Because I give you my word, *Lord* Evander." The duke seethed. "If you have proof to the contrary, then by all means, present it."

Evander's face remained impassive as he studied Iiro for several stilted moments. The tension in the air was suffocating, expanding with every second they stayed in their silent showdown.

Two of the older men in the center whispered back and forth until the one in the red tunic spoke up again.

"We have a way to discover the truth," he declared, calling for one of the guards near the exit. "Fetch Juho."

The clan leaders shuffled in their seats, looking to the man for an explanation until he relented, but not before casting a disdainful glance at me.

I held out my hand, and Iiro absentmindedly dropped my ring into it while he listened to whatever the other duke was saying.

Instead of using the common tongue like before, he spoke in his dialect. Whatever he said had the leaders completely enraptured. Of course, I couldn't understand any of it, so I was completely unprepared when the man they called Juho walked in.

And even more so when the eyes that met mine from the doorway were strikingly familiar.

Der'mo, indeed.

Juho stepped closer with a wicked gleam in his eye, only that's not the name I knew him by.

He had gone by Donal when he worked in our stables back in Lochlann last summer. Though it had been a year, I recognized him immediately. I rarely forgot a face, and certainly not when it was a face that had been firmly planted against mine for the better part of an hour.

The man stepped forward, dipping his head in a small bow toward the duke in red. They went back and forth in their dialect before Donal walked closer to me with a smarmy, knowing expression.

I glared at him. He was a spy. He had infiltrated our home so thoroughly, and I...I had bought every second of the act.

"Princess," he greeted as he neared.

"Traitor," I returned.

Donal, or Juho, rather, laughed before facing the council again.

"Yes, I am *very* familiar with this princess." There was no mistaking his meaning. "She is who he claims she is."

My jaw dropped, my face going as red as my curls. He was making that sound much worse than it was. The arse clown wasn't half as familiar with me as he tried to be.

"Very familiar? I—" I started to snap back at him, but Iiro shot a glare at Theo, who then looked at me with a mixture of warning and pleading in his eyes.

Very well, then.

I shook my head and firmly closed my mouth. Perhaps I should have been relieved that he positively identified me for the council, but knowing the last boy I kissed before Theo was a traitorous spy didn't feel like much of a consolation.

The room erupted into chaos as the dukes began speaking over one another in a combination of the common tongue and their own dialects, all except Evander.

He studied me silently, his calculating gaze the exact shade of the sky just before a storm hits.

A shiver ran through me, and I looked away, unable to bear the weight of his stare. Worse than the noise, though, was when a hush descended, ominous and heavy.

Theo had said the Summit would take days, but maybe this was it. Maybe they were going to order my death here and now.

My heart was pounding in my throat, the anticipation threatening to weaken my knees. But when Iiro spoke, it was four simple, anticlimactic words.

"We will reconvene tomorrow."

CHAPTER 36

Theo and one of the Elk guards flanked me as we followed Iiro back to our tent. Whispers surrounded us at each step, and I wondered how quickly the news would spread about who I was.

And how much more of a target I would be when it did.

Unease hung in the air around us, following us into the tent and refusing to leave, like an unwanted guest. I sank into a chair near the small table, pouring myself a glass of whatever was in the pitcher at the center.

Theo sank down next to me as Iiro spoke to Inessa in Socairan, presumably recounting the events of the day.

I took a long draught of what was most certainly not water, nearly spitting it back out. It was ale, but it was stronger and more bitter than what they served in Lochlann.

"That went fairly well," Theo said, though his voice was tight.

"Ah, yes." I took another tentative sip of the ale,

pleased to find it wasn't nearly as bad when I was expecting the intense flavor. "My favorite part was when they brought in the stableboy I—."

Theo glanced sharply at me, his jaw ticking. "You what?"

I drained my cup before answering, refilling it as I spoke. "It was nothing, just a kiss." *Or several.*

He shook his head, his expression gently exasperated, but his shoulders eased. "In any case, it was only the first day, and it honestly went better than I expected."

I supposed that much was fair, though our expectations for the summit were probably leagues apart. There had been a moment there where I worried they would kill me then and there. So, all things considered...

Theo fiddled with the charm on my bracelet, his fingertips barely brushing my skin.

"I'm just glad this day is finally over," I sighed, leaning my head against his shoulder.

He stiffened. I started to move away but he clamped his arm around my waist.

"Not quite," he said. "There's still the dance."

You have got to be kidding me.

"A dance? To, what? Celebrate my imminent demise?"

I felt his head shake. "It's tradition at the Summit."

I really wanted to tell the Socairans what they could do with all of their traditions at this point, but my protest was cut off by the sound of a familiar voice, breezing in through the tent entrance.

Mila, the young woman from earlier, entered with two servants, each carrying a small trunk.

Her eyes swept around the tent until they found me.

Theo leapt up and put as much distance as possible between us in a way that was too obvious, even for an oblivious person, which I suspected Mila was not.

She arched a perfectly defined brow but said nothing about it, only came to replace Theo's spot on the seat beside me.

"So," she said, drawing out the O sound. "The Scarlet Princess."

A dry laugh escaped me.

"I like the sound of that," I said after a moment. "I see word travels fast."

"They try to pretend the proceedings are a big secret, but it's a fairly small camp." She gestured around. "With literally nothing else to do besides gossip."

The comment reminded me so much of Davin that a physical pang went through me, but I forced a small smile to my lips. At least, until the next words out of her mouth.

"And don't worry, we've all been there with a stableboy or two." She let out a chuckle.

I covered my face with both hands. "You weren't kidding about the gossip."

"It's nothing." She pulled my arm from my face. "Honestly, last summer, my father caught me with one of his guards."

I winced in sympathy. "Did he...kill him?"

"It was a close call, but in the end, he only restationed him. Still, the entire estate heard."

"Not so different from Lochlann after all."

"I wouldn't go that far." She smirked to show she was teasing. "Now, on to more important things. Since I've seen what color your hair is, and your, ahem, shapeliness, I've brought you different gowns."

"That's too much—" I began, though I had to admit I was secretly grateful.

"I have more gowns than I know what to do with." She waved a dismissive hand. "I am happy to share. Besides, my ladies maid already went to the trouble of altering one. You wouldn't want all her work to be in vain?"

She really would give Davin a run for his money.

I laughed, giving in. "Of course not."

"Perfect. Now, we need to get you into a new one for tonight."

"What's wrong with the dress I'm wearing?"

Mila leveled a look at me. "You can't dance in those skirts."

She had a point, but...

"I don't even think I'm going to go," I told her, hoping that was even an option for me. "It's been an exhausting day."

"You have to," she said. "You wouldn't want all those stuffy old men to think they had scared you, would you?"

Another solid point.

"Fine," I relented, and she ordered one of the servants to bring over the trunk.

In spite of myself, an inkling of excitement worked its way through me. There were worse ways to spend the evening than dancing in Theo's arms.

CHAPTER 37

L ike everything in Socair, and really, my life in
general, the dance turned out to be an unmiti-
gated disaster.

Iiro had come to the tent before we left, making sure
that Theo knew not to show me any kind of favoritism. So
not only was I not in Theo's arms, another girl was.
Someone tall and fine-boned and perfectly demure and
Socairan.

I was torn between wanting to stab her and knowing
exactly how unreasonable that was.

It hadn't helped that the atmosphere was desperately
romantic, with lanterns hanging from the trees above us,
glowing like stars and casting a hazy light over the dancers
below.

Though we were outside, it felt as fine as any ball we
would throw back home. Servants carted around trays of
hors d'oeuvres and glasses of some beverage or another. It
was simple, yet grand in its own way.

Mila had also been swept away as soon as we got there,

so I was standing alone on the side of the clearing in my admittedly glorious dress.

It was shimmering gold fabric, tight at the bust and flowing from there for easy movement. The sleeves were long enough to keep me warm in the dropping temperatures, but thin enough that I wouldn't be overheated from the exertion of dancing.

Not that it appeared I would be doing any of that.

I supposed, if things got too boring, I could take out my booby dagger and scandalize the entire camp.

It was a small consolation when half of them couldn't quit staring at me, and the other half seemed to be doing their damnedest to pretend I didn't exist, except for their not-so-subtle signs to ward against evil.

I shook my head and made my way to a vat of what Mila had called medovukha, ladling myself a serving into a cup and ignoring the way that everyone else scattered when I came near.

Tentatively, I brought the cup to my lips, still wary after the borscht incident. But the drink smelled much like the mead we had back home. Taking a sip, I was pleasantly surprised to find it tasted that way, too, if a bit sweeter.

I took another sip, this one much heartier, and was preparing myself to spend my evening in this very manner when a man in red and white robes approached and asked me to dance.

His features and long gray beard were familiar, but it took me a moment to place him as the duke of Ram, the one who had called for Juho earlier. I looked around for some sign of how to proceed only to find Iiro staring pointedly at me from over Inessa's head, giving me a slight dip of his chin.

All right, then.

I gave my hand to the duke, and he led me out to the floor. The dance wasn't much different from the ones in Lochlann, and I caught on easily.

Like sparring, dancing was all about foot movement and reading your opponent, both of which came fairly naturally to me. And this duke was not difficult at all to predict.

He wanted something from me. The only question was *what*?

"So," he began in a thickly accented voice, "you travel alone with only your guard often?"

I blinked at him. "I hadn't intended to be *traveling*."

He gave a gruff noise in the back of his throat that might have been an acknowledgement or a disagreement. "Surely, a princess is not promised to a guard."

"No..." I trailed off, wondering where he was going with this.

Looking for a way to impugn my honor? Juho had done that quite effectively already.

But his hand traveled lower, past the small of my back, pulling me closer.

I wondered if hiking up my skirts to go for my dagger would be considered amicable *or* accommodating?

"My wife died just last year." His breath was warm on my face.

"How very unfortunate." For him, and for me at this moment.

I tried to keep the disgust from my features at where he

was going with this. I needed at least five clans on my side for the final verdict to go my way, but I wasn't sure I wanted to live if it meant sharing a marriage bed with this man.

Perhaps if the alternative was being set on fire?

He cleared his throat, coughing up a wad of phlegm onto the ground next to us.

Nope. Not even then.

"I am sorry for your loss," I tacked on when the silence had gone on for too long. At least I could try not to outright offend him into voting against me.

"Yes," he agreed. "But perhaps something good can come of it."

Then again, maybe I don't care how he votes.

"Oh?" It was all I could say as he spun me around and pulled me in closer than before.

I couldn't help but long for the Lochlannian Court, where Mac or my father would have swooped in if they saw a Lord getting too handsy. Better yet, Avani had been known to send the palace animals in for a well-timed bite.

I almost laughed at the memory before I remembered where I was and who was touching me.

Thankfully, the dance called for a switching of partners before the despicable man could say more, and I found myself thrust into a different duke's arms. Wolf, judging by the insignia on his lapel.

A subtle sigh of relief escaped me. But it was short-lived.

"My son died in the war to defend Clan Bear's honor," the new man spat. "I will enjoy watching you face the noose."

At least he didn't want to marry me. Was this better? Worse? I couldn't decide.

"Thank you for your honesty?" There really was nothing else I could say to that, though this duke didn't look pleased by my response.

The next few dances were much of the same, passing from one ill-intentioned Socairan to another. A few were gentlemen, including Mila's father, and there was more than one that refused to dance with me at all, jumping back from my hair as though it were live spiders rather than harmless crimson curls.

Inessa's father, the duke of Clan Viper, was only barely cordial. Remembering her vague references to the war, I suspected he, too, had cause to hate my people. And therefore me.

Meanwhile, the girls in Theo's arms laughed and simpered, and Iiro watched over me with his commanding glare, daring me to say no to anyone who asked me to dance.

I was beyond finished by the time Lord Evander's hand appeared in front of me, which was the only excuse I had for what popped out of my mouth next.

"Ah, another upstanding gentleman coming to *feel out* the Lochlannian princess." I kept some semblance of an artificial smile plastered to my face for show, even as I sulkily threw my hand in his.

His lips twisted in disgust. "I can assure you, that's the furthest thing from my mind."

I was a bit offended by his revulsion, in spite of myself. It was probably the hair. Maybe I could twirl around too fast and accidentally hit him in the face with the full force of my curls.

Yes. I think I shall.

"So, what, then? You didn't get your fun in calling me a fraud in front of the entire Summit. Now you want to dance?"

He raised a single black eyebrow, his posture relaxing as he placed one hand on my waist.

"I wouldn't go right to *want*." True to his word, his hand didn't stray, his fingers only the barest pressure on my waist.

"Yet, here we are."

"Haven't you noticed that Socairans live and die on decorum?" The corner of his mouth turned up into a cruel smirk. "Quite literally, in your case."

My lips parted in fury. "And now you're mocking me? Do you think it's funny that I might die at the end of this week?"

"Come on, Princess," he sounded bored. Irritated, even. "We both know it won't come to that."

I shot him an incredulous look. "*We* don't know any such thing."

He spun me, waiting until I had returned before speaking again.

"Don't pretend to be naive," he chided. "It doesn't look good on you."

My hand curled into a fist, bunching the fabric at the neck of his tunic. He had what one of my thieving uncles would have called backpfeifengesicht. *A punchable face.*

"I'm not pretending to be naive any more than you're *pretending* to be an arsehole."

He raised both eyebrows this time. "No? So you aren't scheming with the ever-crafty Lord Iiro?"

I wished Davin were here with one of his scathing remarks right about now, but it was just me and my unexpected bout of rage.

"Scheming for what? The illustrious opportunity to put my life in the hands of a group of men who won't so much as let me speak on my own behalf?"

Lord Evander studied me as though searching for the lie, finally shaking his head in disgust. Obviously, he didn't believe that I wasn't in on whatever mysterious plan he had concocted in his mind.

And I was through.

Stumbling quite intentionally, I came down hard on his foot with my heel. He grunted in pain, but didn't falter, and I smiled sweetly up at him.

He narrowed his eyes, murder in his gaze, and I braced myself for whatever cruel thing he was about to say next.

But it was a different voice that sounded in my ear.

CHAPTER 38

"I believe it is my turn," Theo growled.

I had been so caught up in my mounting anger that I hadn't noticed his approach. I nearly sagged in relief, and this time, the feeling stayed.

Evander's fingers tensed around my hand, his eyes narrowing as he met Theo's. But he dropped my hand before they could draw any attention with their silent standoff.

"It has been...enlightening, Princess." Evander sketched a mocking bow before turning to walk away.

Theo's hands swept over me, his warmth searing into the skin on my hand and at my back. I took a deep breath, grateful to be in his arms again, and let him lead me across the twinkling dance floor.

I was finally in his arms, and yet, his body was taut with tension.

"You could have come sooner, you know." I glared up at his warm hazel eyes, a stark contrast to Evander's cold, stormy ones. "Truly, I wouldn't have minded."

Theo's shoulders relaxed a little at my tone, the corner of his mouth struggling not to pull back in a smile.

"It was necessary for them to meet you," he said, gently spinning me away from him and pulling me back in. "Even if I wanted to be the one who had the first dance."

His thumb grazed my ribs in a subtle movement, sending warmth flooding to my center.

"You seemed awfully distracted with your own dance partner." I arched a brow.

He twirled me around in time with the music before letting go of my hands. Two lines of dancers were formed, and we waited on opposite sides while several couples danced between us.

Theo's jaw twitched, and an uncomfortable expression crossed his features as he stared at me over their heads.

When our hands met again, he pulled me even closer, his deep voice reverberating through his chest to mine as he spoke low enough for only me to hear.

"Did that bother you?" He sounded somewhere between baffled and amused.

"Of course not," I lied.

"Really?" He hummed thoughtfully. "Because you seem bothered."

"I am the least bothered person in the world. In fact, I was thinking of dancing four more dances with Lord Timofey, myself. I'm sure he would be happy to accommodate." I glanced suggestively toward the aging duke of clan Eagle.

Theo sighed and shook his head in disapproval, but I didn't miss the amusement that danced in his eyes.

We were swaying peacefully to the lilting music when

the hair on the back of my neck rose. I looked around until my eyes snagged on Lord Evander at the edge of the makeshift dance floor, openly glaring at me.

I scowled back, but his expression didn't shift. He didn't even bother to look away in shame.

Aggravation swept through me until I forced myself to look back at Theo. He must have noticed the brief exchange because he turned us so that I no longer had to face the arseling lord of Clan Bear.

When the music came to a lull, a sign the song was almost over, I spoke again.

"Can we go back to our tent now?"

He froze, a carefully neutral expression taking over his features, and I belatedly realized how that sounded.

Well, I'm in this now.

"I only meant the tent that we share. That we sleep in. Together." A smirk tugged at my lips as I anticipated his adorable blush.

But to my utter surprise, Theo broke into laughter, the sound warm and rich and reverberating through every part of me.

"Storms, Rowan. I suppose I should just feel fortunate that you save all your inappropriate commentary for me."

I thought back to what I had said to the Bear Lord, giving Theo a wan smile. "Indeed, you are."

CHAPTER 39

S adly, we could not go back to our tent.

When Theo asked Iiro about leaving early, his brother insisted we stay for several more dances, all of which Theo danced with someone else.

If I hadn't known any better I would have thought he was trying to punish me.

Even Mila took a turn being his partner, not that I faulted her. She wasn't any more friendly with him than she was with any of the other lords.

I was left waiting for them to finish while standing at the refreshment table. Which, if I was being honest with myself, wasn't the worst thing in the world when there were trays stacked with chocolates and bacon-wrapped bits of goat cheese.

Maybe Iiro knew I would find a way to console myself after all.

I nodded my head to him, raising one of the bacon cheese squares in salute, and I could have sworn there was a hint of a smile tugging at the corner of his mouth when he shook his head in response.

When Iiro finally gave me his permission to leave, Mila danced over to me.

"Come to the sauna with me before bed," she said.

"The what?" I looked at Theo for an explanation.

"It's where we bathe. I went this morning while you were still sleeping."

"Oh." A bath did sound nice. "That sounds perfect, actually."

Theo opened his mouth to say something, but Mila spoke up, making me like her even more. "Don't worry, Lord Theodore. One of my guards can accompany us."

His shoulders were still tense, but he looked to Iiro, who nodded. "All right, then."

It felt awkward, somehow, just walking away from him. I gave him a little wave that only intensified that feeling before turning to leave with Mila. As I had sensed, the air was getting colder by the minute. Not freezing, but certainly colder than the clear day had been before.

I hoped the bath would be warm, at least.

Mila led me to two tents with openings that faced each other, and a walkway lined by semi-opaque material that stretched between them. They were illuminated only by the silver moonlight, the nearest torches several feet away.

She turned to look at her guard, and he stopped, standing outside the makeshift walkway. Near him was a keg next to a table with several steins on it.

Mila filled two cups, handing one to me. "For the sauna," she said, as if that explained everything.

Then she led us into an opening in the fabric walkway, heading first to the tent on the left. It was little more than piles of clothes and towels, and I shot her a quizzical look.

"This is where we undress," she told me. I nodded.

None of this made any sense at all, but I followed her lead anyway, wondering if this was what Theo had opened his mouth to say when Mila cut him off.

She gestured for me to turn around, and we both put our ale down so she could help me out of my dress. I was still unsure of what was going on, but I dutifully recipro-cated, then took off my shift, quickly covering myself with one of the towels.

She was in no such hurry, making me feel like a bit of a prude. Something I never expected in Socair, of all places.

When she left the tent for the walkway, I saw the reason for the low lighting around it, and was eternally grateful for it. She strode through completely nude while I followed in my small towel, hoping that we weren't visible through the thick veils on either side.

The tent on the other side was completely closed, not even an open flap, and up close, I noticed the material around it was thicker than the others.

"Go in quickly when I open it," she said.

I nodded, getting more confused by the minute. Then she unhooked one side of the opening and a cloud of steam rushed out to meet us. Mila grabbed my wrist and tugged me behind her, shutting the flap again.

It was so hot.

So hot.

I could barely see between the low lighting and the

steam filling up the entire tent, but apparently, whoever was in there could see me. Gasps rang out, and I saw the vague outlines of movement.

Mila pulled me until I was sitting on a warm bench.

"Where are the baths?" I whispered.

Before she could answer me, several bodies moved past us, each of them whispering something to the other in Socairan.

The tent entrance being open for so long allowed much of the steam out, enough for me to see that there were no tubs, just a cookpot hanging over a small fire, and a bucket of water with a ladle in it.

Wooden benches lined either side of the tent, made of cedar, if the sweet scent was anything to go by.

I turned to Mila to question her, but she was glaring at the women leaving, the ones I had clearly driven away. "Small minds," she muttered loud enough for them to hear.

They didn't react, just shuffled faster from the tent.

"It's fine," I told her. "I'm used to it." Maybe I hadn't been used to being treated like a leper before coming to Socair, but in the week I'd been here it had become familiar rather quickly.

"It's really not," she countered, agitation coating her tone. Fortunately, she dropped the matter after that.

Two brave souls stayed in the tent near the cookpot, and I realized with a start that they were completely naked, their towels neatly folded next to them. Mila was doing the same at my side.

She caught my expression unabashedly. "Your towel

will get dirty if you leave it on." Her voice was gentle, but matter of fact.

She wasn't wrong, either. Already, sweat was pooling on my forehead and chest, rolling down my body in rivulets.

All right, then.

I pulled my towel out from under me and folded it onto the seat next to me. It wasn't that I was unaccustomed to being nude in front of people, ladies maids and my sisters. But usually, everyone wasn't naked at the same time, or casually visiting as the two ladies at the end were.

Clearly, I was the only one fazed by that, though.

"So," I struggled to take a breath in the oppressive heat. "Are saunas always...a group activity?" I asked.

Mila's laughter echoed throughout the tent. "Just be glad this one is women only. Men and women sauna together in most clans, but the Summit separates them for the few who don't."

"Isn't that...awkward? What if you ran into—" I dropped my voice. "The guard?"

She shrugged. "It would be nothing we hadn't all seen before."

That was one way of looking at it, I supposed. Though the thought of running into Theo in the sauna—I abruptly cut off that line of thought before I turned even redder than the heat accounted for.

Mila stood up, striding over to the bucket and ladling water onto the rocks. A fresh wave of sweltering steam went through the tent.

"What are you doing?" A note of panic crept into my voice.

She laughed again. "They let the steam out."

"I think I already can't breathe." I took a sip of my ale, willing it to cool me down.

"You can, I promise. It's good for your lungs." She added another ladleful, and I wondered idly if anyone had ever actually died in these tents or if I would be the first.

Look at me, doing the Summit's job for them.

Searching for a distraction, I returned to our earlier conversation when Mila sat back down. "Isn't this at odds with how modest you are normally?"

She tilted her head. "I never really thought about it. The saunas are sort of, separate from the rest of society. Being completely nude in an area where you go to be cleansed is practical, but wearing revealing clothing is considered intentional and inappropriate."

I didn't quite understand it, but then, every culture had its quirks.

"Well, we certainly can't have anyone being intentionally inappropriate," I murmured.

She let out another peal of easy laughter, going on to tell me more about Lynx lands and all the fun of being the only girl with four older brothers. Just when I thought I might actually keel over, she got to her feet.

"Are you hot yet?"

"I've been hot from the moment we set foot in this tent," I assured her.

"Good," she said. "Because it's time to rinse off in the river."

I gaped at her. "It has to be freezing this time of year!"

"It's good for you to switch," she insisted. Then, with a look at my hair, she tacked on, "And I think you'll want to do something about that."

My hand went automatically to my curls, which were, indeed, poofier than I had ever felt them, layering twice as high as they should be to create what felt like a giant sphere around my head.

Well, then. I shrugged, putting on a brave face. "When in Socair..."

CHAPTER 40

Whatever bravery I had found evaporated when I stuck a single toe into the icy river.

It was bad enough when I realized we had to make the short trek from the tent to the river in only our towels, no cloth walkway to bar any prying eyes. Fortunately, aside from the guard who kept a respectful distance, we hadn't run into anyone.

"You know, I think I'm cooled down enough already," I said.

"Just covered in sweat," Mila agreed cheerfully.

Her guard turned his back, and she hung her towel on a branch, impervious to the fact that the sparse line of autumnal trees offered plenty of lines of sight to her. She plunged into the calm river without another moment, splashing me in the process.

As soon as she resurfaced, she looked pointedly at me, her face only half visible with the position of the moon. "The longer you wait, the colder it will be," she taunted in a singsong voice.

I knew she was right, about the sweat and the cold. Taking a deep, fortifying breath, I hung my towel next to hers on the branch and stepped to the edge of the river bank. Still, I hesitated.

Until a commotion from further down the river caught my attention, along with a smattering of male voices. Silvery moonlight glinted off a muscled backside, and my jaw dropped.

If I could see them, and my skin was several shades lighter... In fact, I was probably glowing, like a beacon in the moonlight.

That was all the incentive I needed to rush forward into the river. It dropped off more steeply than I expected, and I went under before I kicked off the lower bank to the surface.

I was right. It was freezing.

But also, strangely exhilarating. I felt both cleaner and more awake than I had in days. Weeks, even. Laughing, I swam around a bit more, letting the cold seep inside me and chase away the intense heat of the sauna.

We stayed in the river until we couldn't stand it anymore. Well, until I couldn't stand it anymore. Mila looked like she could have swam in there all night. Seeing her, the way she was happy and outspoken and free, for the first time, I wondered if there was a side of life in Socair that I wouldn't have hated.

THEO WAS WAITING UP WHEN I RETURNED TO THE TENT, though Iiro and Inessa had gone to bed.

"How was sauna-ing?" he asked.

For some reason, instead of the heat of the tent and the freezing cold river, all I could think about was the moonlight revealing sights I could never unsee.

"Fine. Great," I answered. "I'm just going to change into my nightclothes."

"Do you need—"

"No!" I said a little too loudly. "Mila left my laces loose." I disappeared into the other section of the tent before he could see my thoughts playing across my face. By the time I changed clothes, I hoped I could stop awkwardly picturing him in the sauna.

With other women.

Mila had said it was separate, innocent. So why did it make me feel so flustered? Or was I only embarrassed to be thinking about it at all?

It took me longer than it should have to find a night-gown in the chest Mila had left because it wasn't layered and ruffled and awful. In fact, the soft, cream-colored fabric was lacy and pretty, though still modest enough that I didn't have to feel uncomfortable with Theo there.

Mila might just be one of my favorite people in the entire world right now.

CHAPTER 41

The first official day of the Summit was not going well.

Unless I considered a bunch of pontificating old bastards arguing over the best way to kill me "well."

Though perhaps this was how they always went. It was difficult to say, but there was a great deal of shouting and interrupting, and not a small amount of clamoring for my death.

So, all in all, just another typical day in Socair.

I still didn't understand why they required my presence in the tent when I wasn't allowed to speak up or defend myself. Iiro gave implicit instructions that I was only permitted to respectfully answer direct questions, and to keep my features neutral.

Apparently, my face was too expressive...

Seven more days of this was going to be torture.

We had been sitting at the semi-circle shaped table for well over three hours going over the different versions of the same conversation again and again. I watched the dust dance within the beams of light streaming in from the opening in the tent above us, trying to keep my expression under control.

And given the nonsense they were spewing out, I was rather proud that I hadn't made a single face, yet.

"All those who died because of her parents being reckless and giving no thought to anyone but themselves, and here she is, the very same," Sir Nils, the duke from Wolf who had threatened me last night, said. "Let us just be done with her."

"And start a war with Lochlann?" Mila's father, Sir Arès, protested.

"What can Lochlann do to us here, through a single mountain pass, when every man we have is trained and we will have the advantage of familiar lands." This from the one who had proposed an arrangement, Sir Mikhail.

Interesting. I shot him a pleasantly befuddled smirk, which he promptly ignored.

"Perhaps they couldn't win, but surely none of us would volunteer to be the sacrificial lamb before they are eliminated." Arès looked pointedly at Evander, who was too busy glaring between Theo and Iiro to notice.

"They would not make it through the pass with Clan Bear there, and we would lend our forces," the leader of Bison chimed in.

Sir Timofey of Clan Eagle spoke in Socairan, and I had no way of knowing which side he was speaking for.

"Regardless," Lord Evander finally spoke up from the chair closest to my left. "It would be at great cost to us, gaining us nothing in return. Why bother killing her when we can ransom her instead? Lochlann has both goods and money."

"You want to send her home unharmed after what her family did to yours?" Sir Nils sounded offended at the prospect.

"That is precisely why I want to leverage this situation," he answered in a bored tone. "Haven't we all suffered enough at the hands of *them*?"

Sir Mikhail scoffed. "This is why your father should have come himself. He has never been so soft he would shy away from war, or vengeance."

Lord Evander's features turned to ice. "My father couldn't be bothered with these trivialities, and frankly, I don't blame him. Surely eight days is excessive for a single girl."

"Not just any girl," Mikhail shot back.

And so on it went.

When two of the lords started arguing in Socairan, the expressions getting crueler and more heated, I turned to Theo with a questioning look. He gave the barest shake of his head, and his features could have been carved from marble for all they gave away.

Was that good? Bad?

"Don't worry, Princess." Evander shot me a cruel smirk as he leaned toward me, keeping his voice just above a whisper. "They're only debating whether to send your limbs back to your family one by one or just a vial of ashes."

My fingers suddenly felt numb, but I forced my features into amusement. "Surely that first option would get rather expensive, what with all the costs associated with that many messengers," I murmured under my breath. "Not to mention time-consuming. And honestly, who's going to volunteer to travel six weeks or more with a rapidly decaying limb?"

The lord from Clan Bear blinked, his lips parting in surprise.

"And the ashes, well, those could belong to anyone or anything," I went on just as quietly. "Honestly, I expected more from a nation of barbarians. Do feel free to tell me if something more interesting comes up, though.".

I wasn't about to let the arseling know how much his words had bothered me. To even imagine such a thing happening to my parents because of me...well, it was unthinkable.

I ignored him after that, focusing my attention back on the rest of the table. The clan leaders continued to discuss my fate in two languages, forcing me to wonder, was it better to have your gruesome death painstakingly spelled out for you or to be kept in the dark?

Decisions, decisions.

CHAPTER 42

By the time we made it back to our camp, it was as if the day's proceedings hadn't occurred at all, at least not for the people strolling down the roadways in their finest clothes.

Then again, the Summit hadn't been assembled to determine their lives, only mine.

I rubbed my temples, trying not to dwell on the things I couldn't change. I had never been that person, and starting now just felt...masochistic.

Although, it had been a long day of the clan dukes talking about my death like it held no more weight or importance than last night's dessert.

I could practically hear Davin's running commentary in my head, telling me that it was still better than day four in the caves. And he wouldn't have been wrong. At least at the Summit there was food and Theo to comfort myself with.

Taking a glance around, I watched families and friends

gather around the cookfires of each camp. A pang of longing went through me.

I had never been away from my entire family like this. Always, my parents or my sister or one of my cousins or many aunts and uncles, someone was with me. Usually, it was me and Davin. My sister and I were close, but Davin was my best friend.

And now I was here, as close to being alone as I ever had been.

If it weren't for Theo and Mila, would I have sunken entirely into despair, like Avani did?

Physically shaking those thoughts away, I took a deep breath. There was no use worrying about what I couldn't change, and I'd be damned if I spent my last few days of life thinking about death.

I tilted my head, looking up at Theo next to me, admiring the way his lips moved whenever he spoke. It was hard to believe I had only met him a week ago. In his dungeons.

Theo arched an eyebrow in question, and I breathed out a small laugh.

"I was just thinking about the first time we met."

"The first time you remember? Or our real first meeting, where you threw up all over my boots?"

I barked out a laugh, but stopped when I saw his serious expression.

"You're joking," I began. "That didn't happen." I suddenly felt very unsure of that statement.

Theo shrugged, then shook his head. "Unfortunately, I am not."

I gasped, covering my mouth with my hand.

"Before the soldiers could drug you, you cursed at me and vomited all over me."

My head was shaking, but I couldn't stop laughing.

"You lie. You're just trying to cheer me up."

Theo held up a hand in sincerity and shook his head. "It was actually quite impressive. It was as if you were aiming for me. Like you already knew who I was," Theo added with a wry chuckle.

"Well, that does sound like something I would do," I acknowledged. "No wonder you were so taken with me. How could you resist such charm?"

"Ah, yes. It was quite the struggle," he said before stopping and tilting his head to the side, looking at me in question. "What sort of person feels better when they find out they threw up on someone?"

"The sort that feels like you had it coming. You were in the middle of trying to drug and arrest me, after all."

Theo laughed then, his deep voice warming me all the way down to my toes.

"Why did you drug us? Did you and your men truly quake with fear at the clear display of strength Davin and I presented? Were you afraid my hair would slither out and curse you?" I asked.

Theo rolled his eyes. "If you had been spies, we couldn't very well have shown you the quickest route back to our estate. That would have been too easy."

"Fair enough." I shrugged.

We strode into the tent to find a whispering Iiro and Inessa.

They were sitting at the table in the middle of the open center room, their eyes snapping up to meet ours as soon as we entered. Our laughter died, and Theo stiffened beside me, the somber mood effectively dousing the happier one we had created for ourselves.

I darted a confused glance between the brothers as Iiro nodded toward the exit in a way that clearly meant he wanted Theo to follow.

"I'll be back," Theo promised. "I believe I owe you another dance tonight."

With that, he gave my hand a small squeeze before following Iiro back outside. A sinking feeling filled the pit of my stomach as I watched him leave, and I sighed. It was easier not to allow my mind to wander and overwhelm me when he was here.

I turned back around to speak to Inessa when my eyes snagged on a stunning gown that I had missed before. Hanging on the dressing partition, it looked like liquid sapphires.

Silver thread was woven throughout the gown, accenting the deepest shade of blue, lending the gown a sparkling quality. There were shoes and a headpiece to match, but instead of a hat with a veil that would cover my hair, this one was a shining band that sat up high like one of my tiaras back home.

My eyes roved over the fabric and back to Inessa.

"Lady Mila brought that over for you for the dance tonight," she said, standing to reveal her own shimmering emerald-and-gold gown.

While the colors and brocaded fabric were eye-catching, I mentally thanked Mila for being kind enough to provide me with anything other than the high-necked layers of fabric that Inessa's mother had provided for her.

"It's beautiful," I said as she ushered me behind the partition to change. "But, isn't it a little ridiculous that we're expected to dance after a day of deliberating over my life?"

Inessa's fingers froze in the middle of undoing the laces of my dress, and I felt more than heard the long exhale she let out.

Well done. You've offended her again.

I was torn somewhere between being furious at having to play the part of a dancing marionette for all the men who literally debated dismembering me today, and feeling irritated that I could never seem to go long without saying something offensive to someone.

But before I could settle on either feeling, Inessa's fingers moved again and she was already speaking.

"Our people love to dance," she began, her voice quieter than normal. "When the monarchy reigned, they would hold grand balls every season, and it was a mark of dishonor not to attend."

I stepped out of my dress and she set it to the side, handing me a bowl and cloth to clean up with as she continued.

"They mean a great deal to our people." Her tone was quiet, but edged with steel.

I nodded, and she finished helping me in silence.

When we emerged into the main room where Theo and Iiro had returned, I finally asked the question I had been chewing on. "The people seem to have suffered so much without the monarchy. Why are they so reluctant to put it back together?"

"Aside from the belief that the Obsidian Throne is

cursed?" Iiro raised an eyebrow. "Because they can't decide who they want to lead. Clan Elk is the closest blood relation to the throne. Our mother was the first cousin of the late queen, but Clan Bear believes that their size and brute strength affords them a claim as well."

"That's why it's so important to form alliances," I mused aloud.

And for me to come here, to do this with full transparency. Not only would they have risked losing their allies, but having met Lord Evander, I had no doubt that Clan Bear was cruel enough to retaliate for any perceived slight.

They had gone to war for their pride once already.

I still had no desire to be the sacrificial lamb for the peace of their clans, but I couldn't deny that I understood their predicament a bit better now, the one that I had put them in.

By showing up, a Lochlannian royal breaking their laws, I had forced them to either risk war from their fellow clans by keeping my presence a secret, or risk war on all of Socair if the Summit decided to kill me.

Either way, blood would be shed. Because of me.

CHAPTER 43

A s much as I had been dreading another night of being manhandled and watching Theo dance with other women, Mila's presence made the evening almost bearable with a running commentary on all the clan dukes.

"Oh, it's definitely not real." She giggled into her cup of medovukha. "One year, Sir Danil shows up bald as an egg, and the next he's sporting a full head of what I'm fairly certain is boar's hair." She pointed at the duke of Crane.

"It's a real shame he's taken," I said, laughing into my own glass.

"What about you? Are you *taken*?" Mila wiggled her eyebrows at me.

I feigned a blush. "Why, yes. I have an entire Summit of Socairan dukes vying over me and my future as we speak. If only they weren't also planning my untimely demise."

Mila waved a hand dismissively. "They won't kill you. Our people can be brutal, but rarely have they ever sentenced a woman to death."

For the first time since I woke up in the dungeons, a real spark of hope ran through me, and I tried to stamp it out.

"I don't know, Mila. They are pretty convincing..."

"My father thinks they just want to scare you. I'm sure they'll ransom you back home. At least, that's what he's pushing for." She smiled reassuringly at me.

It was too much to hope for, really.

"Back to more important matters," I said, shaking off the feeling. "Are *you* taken? Or has someone here caught your eye?"

She sighed, her full lips going into a pout. "My father is more lenient than most, but yes. I'll have to marry fairly soon. Probably within my clan, since he wants to remain isolated, which is probably for the best, considering the alternatives."

She cast a glance around the room, barely suppressing a shudder. "The only people with high enough ranking to consider switching clans for are dukes and their heirs. Which, aside from Sir Mikhail, the old pervert in Ram, leaves only Bear and Elk."

My stomach gave a flip at hearing her casually refer to marrying Theo, but I forced it to calm down.

"And you don't want that?"

She leveled a look at me. "I would actually rather die than marry into Clan Bear. My father says they used to be upstanding enough, but since the war, they're...barbarians. No one is safe in their territory, with random raids to slaughter the villagers they deem 'disobedient,' and they attack the other clans at will. They've only managed the alliances they have because everyone is terrified of them.

"And Evander...don't let that pretty face fool you. He's the worst one." She trailed off, her face losing a shade of color.

Looking at the dark-haired lord now, dancing with a bored expression in his cruel gray eyes, I didn't find that hard to believe.

"And...Theodore?" I forced myself to ask.

"Theodore is nice enough, but he's been in talks with Ram forever." She pointed to the woman Theo had been dancing with yesterday. The one who was in his arms at this very moment. "Galina is Mikhail's niece, and she doesn't speak to me because we refused to side with her clan in..."

But I missed the rest of whatever she was going to say. I fiddled with the bracelet he had given me, turning over the lotus charm in my fingers as my heart dropped into my stomach. My voice was sharper than I meant for it to be when I spoke.

"Marriage talks?"

Mila snapped her gaze to mine, something between wariness and apology on her perfect features. She opened her mouth to respond, but we were both cut off by a rather pompous throat clearing.

Lord Evander stood a respectful foot away, extending his hand. "Would you do me the honor of this dance, Princess?" He smirked around the word *honor*, like this was anything but.

"I find I'm quite tired this evening—" I began, but Iiro appeared from out of nowhere.

"Nonsense, Princess Rowan. Weren't you just saying how much you looked forward to *amicably accommodating* your dance partners this evening?"

Why it should matter if I was polite to a clan that was their enemy was beyond me. I sighed.

"Ah yes. I just uttered that very thing to Lady Mila." Sarcasm crept into my tone. "Though, I could never hope to be quite as *amicable* with my dance partner as Lord Theodore has apparently been with his." I added the last bit under my breath, and Mila laughed.

Iiro's mouth flattened into a tight line, and I raised my eyebrows in a small challenge.

The answering warning in his eyes reminded me of everything that was at stake, though, both my life and Davin's. So I spread my lips into a thin veneer of a smile, handing Mila my glass and giving Evander my hand without looking at him.

"You seem especially cantankerous today," the arseling commented as soon as we were on the floor.

Once again, in sharp contrast to the other lords, his hands were barely grazing my waist, the subtle pressure of his fingers my only cue of where he was leading.

"Whereas most people in a farce of a trial for their lives would be celebrating?" My tone was caustic, but I didn't care.

Evander's vote was shot anyway, and from what Mila said, he would scare others into submission. I scowled and turned away, my eyes landing on *Galina*'s shiny locks swaying as Theo twirled her.

The lord followed my gaze, scoffing quietly. "Yes, it certainly seems to be the Summit that is the problem. Has the congenial Lord Theodore actually managed to upset someone?" He said *congenial* like it was a bad thing.

My eyes whipped back to meet his. On the surface, he was attractive enough, with his black wavy locks, stormy eyes, and full lips that were always tilted in amusement at some cruel joke only he understood.

But he had no warmth. No compassion.

I tried to school my expression, but my tone had no such restraints. "Do you think Lord Theodore is soft because he doesn't venture into villages to wantonly murder his own people?"

Evander's gaze darkened. "Order must be maintained, and sometimes that means making a difficult judgment call. Don't worry, Princess. No one here expects you to understand that."

My lips parted in fury, and I nearly stumbled when he turned me in time with the dance.

"And why not?" I asked through gritted teeth when we were together again.

"Because you're a woman." He shrugged. "And because you've lived a life of unimaginable privilege. Hell, you were so bored, you had to go and invent drama for yourself by running along on your smuggling adventure." A bitter laugh escaped him. "And even here, you don't seem to have the sense to be afraid. What would you know of responsibility?"

His words hung in the air between us, his expression daring me to challenge him.

"Well, I apologize, Lord Evander, if I have not

adequately cowered for your entertainment, but I do believe I feel my knees weakening with terror at this very moment. Do excuse me."

With that, I dropped his hand, spun on my heel, and walked away.

CHAPTER 44

I made it all the way to the refreshment table without Evander following me or Iiro chastising me. My face must have displayed every bitter thought running through my mind, because more than the usual amount of people gave me a wide berth.

Giving myself something to do other than stand and stew in my own irritation, I made myself a small plate of the tiny pancakes with cream and a black garnish, along with a skewer with fruit and cheese.

Without too much thought, I popped the entire little pancake in my mouth and instantly regretted it.

The bread part was delicious, but the black garnish made me want to heave. It felt as if I had poured a cup of salt over an old fish and let it congeal in my mouth.

My eye twitched of its own accord, and a shiver ran from my neck down to my toes. Spinning around so that no one could see me, I searched in vain for a napkin to spit it out.

"Dance with me?" Theo's familiar deep voice intoned

from behind and I froze.

With no other options left, I forced myself to chew and swallow the horrid mouthful, and was only just successful at keeping it down. Instead of turning to face him, I ladled myself a glass of medovukha and drank it down as quickly as possible.

When I finally turned to face him, I was relieved to find that he was alone.

"Dance with me?" he asked again. His voice was tenuous, like maybe he knew every vicious thought that had been running through my mind only a few moments ago.

Theo's sincere gaze bored into mine and for a moment, I almost forgot why I had been so upset to begin with. Or perhaps he just saw my queasy expression.

I nodded sharply, finishing off my glass, before setting both it and my plate down on the table and taking his hand.

When the music was at a steady hum, the tension had already begun to ease out of me and I wanted to sink into Theo's arms for the rest of the night.

But then Mila's words came back, and I froze.

Theo tilted his head in a question, and I leaned forward, speaking as quietly as I could.

"Were you promised to someone else before I came here?" It struck me that I had never asked.

He had asked me, but I never reciprocated, and suddenly, I felt foolish for that. What other questions wasn't I asking?

Theo's brow furrowed. "You mean Galina?"

I hated the sound of her name on his lips. *What is wrong with me?* For the few kisses I had shared with the men at court...and a couple of stableboys, I had never been jealous. It was an ugly feeling, clawing its way out from inside me, but I couldn't seem to stop it.

I nodded again.

"We had discussed the possibility of negotiating an alliance," he said as we dipped between the other dancing couples.

"Through marriage?" I clarified.

"Yes, but—"

"Why didn't you tell me?"

Theo's eyes widened, like he was willing me to understand. "Because...nothing was official. It still isn't. And... then I met you."

My stomach twisted.

"Theo, I can't be that girl. I can't have you string her along because of whatever this is between us." I took a breath. "And you know this can't last..."

His hazel eyes bored into mine, and his hand at my waist tightened.

"No, I don't know that," he said, running his thumb back and forth on my side. "But, it also isn't like...that, with Galina. It's only been talks of a possible arrangement. Nothing set in stone. She knows that."

I stole a glance at the girl who was very much staring daggers at me.

"I don't know that she does."

He sighed, irritably this time. "Galina was someone my brother chose for the good of the clan." He leaned closer to me, talking in a low voice in my ear. "But she isn't who I choose."

My heart galloped within my chest. Tension crackled

between us with everything we both refused to say, and I began to feel impossibly stupid about this entire thing.

"Well. You didn't have to dance with her so much," I muttered.

He chuckled softly. "Appearances, remember?"

Right.

"That's really not my strong suit," I said wryly.

He raised his eyebrows in mock surprise. "You don't say."

Not for the first time, I missed Davin. These were his strengths, subterfuge and secrets and all the court games. Mine lie more...well, I didn't actually know where my strengths lie.

Not in good decision-making, and certainly not in politics. I was an average fighter, better than Davin, admittedly, but nothing at all like my cousin, Gwyn.

I supposed I'd have to settle for being amusing and hope that was enough when pitted against Galina's mile-long legs and perfect Socairan lack of personality.

WHEN THE DANCE WAS OVER, MILA CAME TO GRAB ME for the sauna. Theo escorted us over this time, making me promise that we would wait for him to head back to the tents.

This time, I was prepared for the intense heat when we entered the tent. I was surprised to find I even enjoyed relaxing in the dark, steam-filled space with a mug of ale in my hand. It was at least preferable to dancing in front of everyone.

Even the prospect of the freezing cold river afterwards was more appealing than an encounter with Sir Mikhail, and certainly more so than Lord Evander.

Mila chatted about the lords she danced with and whose company she enjoyed more when my attention was pulled to the tent entrance.

Galina's eyes roved over the empty tent until they met mine, and the smile on her elegant face quickly disappeared.

In spite of what Theo had said, I wasn't sure she felt the same way. I saw the way she looked at him when they were dancing, and it wasn't the look of someone who was just *in talks* about a marriage alliance.

She averted her gaze and turned to leave when I called out to her.

"No, we'll go," I said, standing up and polishing off my mug of ale. "The sauna is all yours."

Galina didn't reply, but her shoulders seemed to relax a little when Mila shrugged and followed me out.

Theo's words from the dance came back to me as we dove into the river and again when we were drying off and waiting for him to escort us back.

Galina wasn't his choice.

My chest tightened at the thought with an emotion I couldn't name. I wasn't sure what I should feel or think about that.

She was just a pawn in another man's game.

And with the dukes vying for my hand in marriage or suggesting new and creative ways to leverage me against my family every other hour, that was something I understood all too well these days.

CHAPTER 45

The next day of deliberations was largely the same as the day before.

The pride of the clans was getting the better of them. They were so convinced that Lochlann couldn't touch them here.

I didn't know who would win in a war. I only knew that I didn't want to find out, especially not when my father, Uncle Finn, and Gallagher would be the ones leading it.

After another long day hearing the variety of ways I could and should be killed, Theo led me back to our tent. We passed a sparring ring on the way, this time with swords. Once again, Theo's eyes lit up.

I couldn't help the way the corners of my mouth pulled up into a smile. Seeing him excited about something helped lift the fog from my own mood.

"Go," I said, through a small laugh.

"It's fine. We can walk some more, maybe grab some food from the other carts." Even as he said it, his eyes drifted in the direction of the sparring ring and I shook my head.

"You shouldn't have to miss out just because I'm here. It really is fine. I'll watch from a distance this time."

Theo's mouth tilted in a dubious grimace.

"Safely," I added.

What I didn't say is that we didn't have time to go back to the tent first because a rainstorm was coming, and I couldn't afford to arouse any suspicion by grabbing a cloak with the clear blue sky.

But I would risk a little rain to watch Theo swordfight, especially when the alternative was stewing back in the tent. Alone, most likely, since Inessa spent her days with her family.

Theo visibly warred with himself, and I smiled up at him, reaching out a hand to touch his bicep.

"Would you really deprive me of the chance to see you and all those glorious muscles in action?"

His eyes widened, and red flooded his cheeks as he stepped back. "Princess Rowan! You can't say those things here." He shot furtive glances around, and a giggle escaped me.

"I'll stop if you let me come," I pressed.

Theo ran a hand over his face and shook his head. "Fine, *if* you at least try to be inconspicuous this time. But know that you're impossible."

"Oh, I do know," I said in a cheeky tone, finally eliciting a small grin from him.

He found me a place to sit on a hill just behind the sparring ring. Everyone down by the ring crowded in close, placing bets and cheering on or booing at the competitors.

Though I would have preferred to be closer to the action, I couldn't deny that I liked my vantage point from the hill. It gave me a clearer view of the match than I would have had standing on my tiptoes in a sea of giant men.

When it was Theo's turn, I sat up a little straighter, grinning as he nodded in my direction.

I couldn't help but swoon a little as he took off his shirt, and the fading sunlight caught on the hard ridges of his chiseled abs. He was flawless, like an artist had painstakingly carved every inch of him with precision and care.

The man sparring with him removed his shirt as well, revealing a tattoo of an eagle in flight, the feathered wings spanning all the way from one shoulder to the other. He flexed and lifted his sword in the air.

More boos than cheers rang out, and I wondered if Theo was a favorite or if this man was just unliked.

The man serving as the announcer called for the match to begin, using the common tongue. Theo raised his blade, lightly tapping it against his opponent's to signal the start of their fight.

Eagle immediately took on the offensive and lunged forward, arching his sword to the right before bringing it down quickly. Theo took a step back and met his blade, the sound of scraping steel echoing through the valley.

They tested each other several more times, looking for weaknesses before the fight began in truth.

The man came at Theo with a blur of speed, raining down blow after blow. He was quick on his feet, shuffling around with rapid, darting motions to catch Theo unaware.

But Theo never wavered. He met each thrust of the other man's sword, deflecting with lightning fast speed, never allowing the man an opening, but never attacking, either. After a while, it was clear that the man from Eagle was waning, while Theo was hardly winded.

It was clear that he was gaining the upper hand. At least, it was clear to me.

I was so enraptured watching the powerful arcs of Theo's sword, I nearly missed the crackling awareness of an adversarial presence nearby. Lord Evander approached, a smug grin on his lips.

"My money's on the Eagle." He side-eyed me. "Our Lord Theodore is already being worn down."

I scoffed. "Hardly."

"Care to wager?" He raised an eyebrow as he took a seat next to me.

"You know that I have nothing here that's mine." I rolled my eyes.

"I'm sure I'll think of something," he said smoothly, wrapping his arms around his bent knees.

Was anyone here not a lecher? "Ew. No, thank you."

Now it was his turn to roll his eyes. "Why do you always assume I want that from you? I think I'll add conceited to your list of admirable qualities."

My cheeks reddened, but I said nothing.

"In any case," he went on. "I was thinking more along the lines of answering a question."

So he could ask me something important about my kingdom or Theo's clan? "Still no."

"So you were just being loyal before, then. You don't actually believe Elk is going to win this one?"

"Of course I do." I scowled, pointing to the match. "See, Theodore is baiting him. Eagle is flagging, and Lord Theodore is allowing him to tire himself out on the offensive. He's just biding his time."

We watched as exactly that unfolded. Eagle's blows became slower, and Theo took advantage of that by shifting from parrying to going on the offensive, effectively reversing their roles. Eagle stumbled backward at the onslaught just as they were both shadowed by the ominous clouds rolling in.

"Then what do you have to lose?" Evander taunted.

I glanced away from the fight to look at his smug face. Taking his coin *did* sound appealing right about now. And I only promised that he could ask a question, not that I would answer it. "Fine. Two gold pieces for one question."

"That's an expensive question."

"I have expensive taste." Might as well feed into his image of me as a princess. It wasn't entirely a lie, but mostly I just wanted to take as much as I could.

"All right. Have it your way. I suppose you already know what's going to happen next?"

"Not blow by blow, obviously, but any idiot," I looked at him meaningfully, "can see that Lord Theodore is going to switch it up and feint to the left before delivering the winning blow."

Evander narrowed his eyes at me before turning back to the fight.

Sure enough, within five moves, Theo had successfully knocked the man's sword from his hand, raising the tip of his blade to his opponent's neck. The man's hands went up in surrender and cheers erupted from the crowd.

I held out my hand in Evander's direction. A moment later, he handed over two coins with a sigh.

"I see you were right," he said, but something in his voice was off. Rather than defeated, he sounded distinctly...amused.

Suspicion slithered over me just as the caller in the sparring ring shouted over the roaring crowds.

"...Elk will face off against Bear!"

The air whooshed from my lungs. I shot Evander an accusing look that bounced right off of him.

"Looks like I'm up next," he said with a dry laugh, getting to his feet and walking down the hill. Just before he got to the ring, he turned back and called over his shoulder. "Oh, and thanks for the tips. They should come in handy."

I barely heard the last few words over the furious thundering of my heartbeat drumming in my ears. Here was hoping Theo wiped that stupid smug look off of his face.

CHAPTER 46

I paced the hillside as I racked my brain to remember everything I had said to Evander about Theo's fighting.

Why did I even engage with him to begin with?

Evander kept his shirt on as he grabbed one of the sparring swords and stalked toward Theo in the ring. I reminded myself that Theo was skilled and immensely powerful.

Then why did a small part of me wish the rain would hurry up and come down? Of course, they would probably just fight anyway, if the way they were looking at each other was any indication.

I forced myself to take a deep breath.

There was no way I could have said anything that would have given Evander the upper hand. *Was there?*

Their match began, and I held on to that hope for all of thirty seconds into their match. Right up until Evander glanced up at me and winked.

Son of a...

What is he plotting?

It was an effort to think past the pounding in my skull and the tingling on my spine to assess the match.

The two men really couldn't be more different. Where Theo was a solid force of strength to be reckoned with, Evander was blinding speed and fluid grace. The three times I had witnessed Theo fight before, I had held every confidence in his victory.

Now, though, watching him with Evander made my stomach churn...because he was going to lose.

Logically, I knew this was only a sparring match. It wasn't a real duel. It shouldn't matter.

But it did.

Anyone could see the rivalry brewing between them, a dislike that ran deeper than rivaling clans accounted for.

I held my breath as Theo raised his sword and brought it down hard on Evander's. Instead of meeting his blade, Evander avoided it all together, leaping backward at the last possible second and forcing Theo's strength to be wasted on the ground.

Theo was clearly stunned, but he kept his head enough to dodge Evander's attack that followed just after, bringing his blade up to parry. They continued back and forth like this for what felt like an hour, with Evander using Theo's strength against him and...

My stomach twisted. That filthy bastard had gotten me to give away Theo's strategy and was using it against him. Theo thought it was Evander on the offensive, wearing himself out, that he was just responding. But that was far from the truth.

Evander feinted several times, lunging forward to draw

Theo out. But his blows were clumsier than they should be, and he looked exhausted, overheated, like the last man had been.

The difference was that he was clearly faking, whereas Theo actually was tiring out.

The arsehat allowed Theo to get closer and closer to him, setting him up for a move like the one that gave him his victory before. And Theo walked right into it.

Just like before, Theo switched up his rhythm to throw Evander off before feinting to the left. But instead of falling for it, Evander attacked to the right in an unending frenzy.

I saw red. I had unwittingly been the chink in Theo's armor, and Evander was hacking away at it before my eyes.

His blows were a blur, becoming faster than I could track as he lunged toward Theo, completely off-footing him.

Theo stumbled backward in the rush, and Evander stuck out his foot to finish tripping him. I cringed as he fell to the ground, his grip loosening on the pommel of his sword enough for Evander to knock it out of his grasp, catching it midair.

He rested both swords at the sides of Theo's neck, and a hush fell over the audience.

Their eyes were locked in a silent battle raging between the two of them until several ragged breaths later, Theo raised his hands in defeat.

My fist clenched around the gold coins. They were round and weighty. Perhaps I could choke Evander with them.

Just as I had promised, I dutifully waited on top of the

hill instead of racing down to the ring. Even if it did take every bit of self-control I had ever possessed. Theo fielded a few pats on the backs and comments before heading my way.

As soon as he caught sight of my expression, his pinched in concern.

"What's—" He started to speak, but a wry laugh cut him off.

"I'd say two gold coins was more than a fair price to pay for victory. " Evander called over Theo's shoulder.

Before I could iterate my fury, thunder crackled above us and the sky split open in response, dumping buckets of water on all of our heads. Sounds of shock and alarm rang out, everyone scrambling to get to shelter.

I didn't bother. The pressure I could feel was minimal. This wasn't really a storm, so much as a few clouds of rain at this point. Still, I didn't protest when Theo grabbed my hand and pulled me toward our tent.

Even if it meant we had to leave before I got the chance to stab Evander.

CHAPTER 47

The heavy rains chased us all the way back to the tent.

I was soaked through by the time we made it inside, water drenching every square inch of my cream-colored gown. With the dropping temperatures, I registered that I should be cold, though I was far from it.

My heartbeat pulsed hard enough in my ears that it nearly drowned out the deafening thunder outside. I paced the small space of the tent's main room, growing angrier and angrier with each step.

"He tricked me."

Theo shook the water from his head and began to strip off layers of his wet coat and shirt, hanging them over the dressing divider to dry.

"That's what he always does, Rowan," he said bitterly, grabbing a towel to wipe down. "It's who he is."

"It's still my fault you lost," I said, clenching my fists. "If I hadn't—"

Theo slung his towel over his shoulder, gently placing both of his hands on my arms.

"It wasn't your fault. Evander just likes to get under people's skin. I'm sure he already had his fighting strategy in mind. He just wanted to make you feel bad by making you think you had contributed."

The warmth of his touch seared into me, forcing my body to finally register how cold it actually was. I shivered and leaned further into him.

"How very upstanding of him," I muttered, my fury dampening a smidge.

"That's just Clan Bear." Theo sighed. "Don't let him get to you. It was only a sparring match." He sounded like he was convincing himself as much as me, only worsening my guilt.

I took a deep breath and slowly blew it out, meeting his golden green eyes. It wasn't like me to get so angry, let alone stay that way. Turning around, I gestured for him to undo the laces of my dress, trying and failing to calm myself in the process.

When he was finished, I moved to the other side of the divider and peeled the wet dress from my body, along with my shift, and patted myself dry with one of the spare towels.

"It's just frustrating, knowing that he's so conniving and he seems to be against you in every way." When I was done drying off, I slipped into the nightgown I had left there earlier. I would have to change again later, but for the moment, it was warm and dry. "Not only could he cost me my life, but after meeting him, I don't trust that he won't try to bring war to your doorsteps just for his claim to the throne."

I came back to the main room to find Theo lacing up a dry pair of trousers, still shirtless. My eyes snagged on the motion, and I looked away, rambling in my discomfort.

"Mila told me about how they treat their people on his lands. The thought of their clan being in control of all of Socair... I just—"

Theo came closer to me, lifting my chin with a calloused finger and pressing his lips to mine. It was ridiculous how much I had missed this feeling after going only a few days without it. I melted into the touch, savoring every second of the momentary distraction.

When he pulled away a fraction of an inch, his words were a whisper across my mouth.

"I can deal with Evander. Don't worry. The other clans would never tolerate a war for that." He leaned in again, planting a chaste kiss on my nose. "I think you should know that you are adorable when you're angry."

His lips pulled back in one of those rare smiles he reserved for me, and the last vestiges of my anger evaporated.

"Well, that's something, at least." I smirked. "I've heard that being adorable covers a multitude of sins."

His grin widened, making my heart race for entirely different and far more inviting reasons than it had been earlier.

"I think I know something that might put you in a better mood," he added, tucking an unruly strand of hair behind my ear. "If it keeps raining, the dance tonight will be cancelled."

"Darn, and I was so looking forward to dancing with Sir Mikhail again."

I said and Theo shook his head, a wry chuckle reluctantly escaping his lips. "Whatever will we do to pass the time?"

His bare chest rose slowly, and his gaze darkened.

"I'm sure we'll come up with something." He arched a brow and leaned in further, wrapping an arm around my waist to bring my body flush against his.

In several tauntingly slow seconds, his mouth met mine once again. My hands made the slow trek up his torso, widening out to explore the corded muscles of his broad shoulders.

He made a sound low in his throat, and I fisted my fingers in his short blonde locks, pulling him even closer down toward me. His hands traced a proprietary arc down my shoulders, around my waist and lower, exploring the swells of my hips and brushing along the outside of my thighs.

He pulled me into our section of the tent, laying me down on the bedroll without breaking our kiss. Then he was balanced over me, his lips skating from my mouth, down my jaw, over to the sensitive area below my ear.

His fingers grazed my skin in tantalizing movements, but he never took it any further than that. I was grateful for that, when things were complicated enough as it was.

For a while, there was only Theo. His lips, his tongue, his breath mingling with mine. Nothing and no one else existed outside of this space we had carved out for ourselves.

NIGHT HAD FALLEN AT SOME POINT WHILE THEO AND I were wrapped up in each other. I reluctantly pulled away from him when Inessa and Iiro returned, using the excuse of needing the privy.

When I returned, he was already in his bedroll. It felt ridiculous that we were so far apart in the small space when all I wanted to do was be near him, but even I had more propriety than that.

So I reluctantly got into my own bedroll, pulling the blankets around me, and Theo turned out the lantern. There were several beats of silence before he sucked in a breath to speak.

"Have you given any thought at all to what you'll do after the Summit?" he asked.

"It's starting to feel like there won't be an 'after the Summit' for me." I meant it as a joke, but it fell flat.

"Hey," he said softly. "That won't happen. Several of the clans are in favor of ransom or sending you home, and all we need is five."

I let his words wash over me. "Here's hoping."

"But if they do. You'll...go home, to Lochlann?"

"When the pass is open," I responded softly.

Silence stretched between us again, and once more, he was the one to break it.

"Have you considered whether you would want to stay here?" His tone was hesitant, almost as if he had been nervous to ask.

"You mean...with you?" I forced myself to clarify.

"Well, certainly not with Sir Mikhail," he said drily.

I let out a surprised huff of laughter. "Honestly, I hadn't thought about it." Realizing how that sounded, I winced. "I mean, I haven't given much thought to anything past the Summit. That's as far as I can see right now."

"And if you did think about it?"

I swallowed uncomfortably. This was the last conversation I wanted to have right now, but after spending the entire evening with my lips pressed against his, I probably owed him an answer.

"Did you know that my sister was married?" I asked.

If he was surprised by my abrupt question, he didn't show it. "Yes."

"Then you also know that he died?" Somehow it was easier to talk about this in the dark, where he couldn't see my features.

"Yes." His voice held more sorrow this time.

"We grew up with Mac. He was like a brother to me, but to Avani...he was her everything. And when he died, it was like a part of her died with him."

The back of my eyes burned unexpectedly, my longing for my sister so visceral, it was like a palpable thing. I missed her so much, and now I may never see her again.

Now, she may lose me too.

"I'm sorry," Theo said, pulling me from my thoughts, but it was clear in his tone he hadn't connected the dots. So I tried again.

"My aunt and uncle helped start a war with their love. My parents may have won our people over in the end, but there were years when the people and the Council didn't quite trust them because they hid their relationship." I sighed. "The thing is, I never wanted to marry for love. I never wanted to be in love. I still don't want that for myself."

Several moments passed wherein I was sure Theo hated me. Not being able to see his expression was torture. Then I heard movement, and I squinted to make out the shadowed outline of his form stepping out of his bedroll.

He was so upset, he was walking away. I had a small moment of panic, wondering what I could say to soften the blow that wasn't an outright lie.

But instead of leaving, he pulled his bedroll closer to mine, laying down on top of the blankets. He moved closer to me, his face inches from mine when he finally spoke.

"You love me?"

My mouth opened, then closed, before I finally responded. "That's not what I said."

But had I been thinking it, somewhere in the back of my head?

"I think it is." There was amusement in his tone, but on the bright side, at least my humiliation could kill me before the Summit had a chance.

"That would be ridiculous," I whispered. "We've only known each other for ten days."

"Hmm. Then I guess I'm ridiculous, too."

I stopped breathing. "You don't mean that. You can't fall in love with someone in ten days."

"No, not ten days. It only took me two." He sounded so much more casual than his words were.

"Liar." My voice was quiet.

"No." He trailed his fingers from my wrist to my elbow and back again, tracing a figure eight pattern as he spoke. "From the moment I heard you laugh in my dungeons, I had to know what kind of person could light up such a dark place. I was completely captivated by you. I found myself coming up with excuses to be around you."

I thought of him finding me and giving me a tour instead of sending me back to my rooms, and I knew there was some truth to that.

"Captivation isn't love," I pointed out.

"No," he acknowledged. "But when you put yourself in more danger to keep Davin safe, when you showed concern for my people even though they were unkind to you, even seeing you laugh with Mila. It's impossible not to love you."

I had no words to respond to what he was saying, no way to explain how hearing him say that made me feel, so I closed the distance between us and pressed my lips against his.

He moved until he was hovering over me, one solidly muscled arm propping him up on either side, then lifted his head back enough to murmur against my mouth. "And Rowan?"

"Mhmm?"

"Just so you know, I think that loving someone is a terrible reason not to marry them. Of all the ridiculous things you've ever said, that might be the worst."

I let out a small laugh. "Worse than weather toe?"

He pretended to deliberate, making a humming noise in the back of his throat. "No." His mouth connected with mine again in a quick kiss. It was playfully loud, and I couldn't even bring myself to care that Inessa and Iiro probably heard it. "Nothing will ever be more ridiculous than weather toe."

In my head, I knew that he was right, but I couldn't bring myself to want to belong so completely to another person like that.

Even if I couldn't bear the thought of never seeing him again.

He kissed me again with more urgency this time, like he could hear the direction of my thoughts. I responded in kind, trying to drown out all the doubts and worry about what the future held.

For now, we just needed to get through the next five days.

CHAPTER 48

As it turned out, that was easier said than done.

The third and fourth days of deliberations slipped by in a haze of threats and increasingly macabre ways to use me against my family, followed by some very unappealing offers at the evening dances.

At least the nighttime offered some reprieve. Theo still hadn't moved his bedroll back, and every night I fell asleep with his hand on mine after a flurry of stolen kisses.

Still, even that wasn't enough to distract me from the very real possibility of my death in three short days.

So far, Clans Lynx and Viper were allied firmly with Elk, while Eagle and Bison argued vehemently against it. We all knew where Bear stood, and that left three clans floating somewhere in the middle, occasionally arguing on both sides of the issue.

Until the fifth day.

Until the moment that Sir Mikhail from Clan Ram, the same duke who had twice now suggested that he could be *persuaded* to change his vote for the low price of my body and my hand in marriage, spoke up again in defense of my death.

"If the girl dies, King Logan himself will come," Inessa's father argued, not for the first time.

"Let him come," Sir Mikhail said. "We can easily outnumber their forces here, and then the castle will be ripe for the taking. And so will the heir to the throne." He leered when he said it.

Fear shot through me, numbing my fingers with its intensity, and white-hot fury followed on its heels. I had listened with increasingly stony silence as the various means of my death were described at length, but this time, they went too far.

This time, they threatened my sister.

"Need I remind you what happened the last time someone attacked a castle my mother was defending?" My voice held nothing but lethal calm, the still tension of a mountain lion just before it goes in for the kill. "And tell me, how many people needlessly died when you came against my father's forces, when you convinced yourself you had a reason to go to war."

Audible gasps sounded around the room.

Meanwhile, Iiro looked like he might murder me, and Theo's eyes widened in horror. I ignored them all.

My body trembled with the force of my rage, and I realized that if the Summit was going to vote against me anyway, I sure as hell wasn't going down as some silent, *de-stars-damned-mure*, lady.

I met each of their eyes in turn, cataloging looks of

fury and disdain and a cruel sort of amusement—that last one on Lord Evander, of course.

"If you're going to kill me, get on with it, but don't fool yourselves." A low laugh escaped my lips, but there was no humor in the sound. "You are no match for anyone in my family, least of all my mother, and sure as hell not my sister."

Avani would have an arrow through the eye of every man who tried to come near her. I almost wanted to see them try.

Instead of responding to me, Duke Mikhail looked at Iiro, narrowing his eyes.

"Our clans have been considering our alliance because Ram respects your strength. But I'm not sure that is the case anymore," he seethed. "It seems, these days, you cannot keep a single girl in check."

Iiro flushed with fury, but his voice was calm when he spoke. "I think that's enough deliberation for now."

I got to my feet and stalked out of the tent without asking for their permission or waiting to see how they would respond. Whatever I had just done, I couldn't undo it now. Maybe it would give them something to think about, for a change.

Maybe they could all go straight to hell.

Footsteps followed me urgently, crunching on the fallen leaves, but I didn't turn around until Theo's voice sounded behind me.

"Rowan," he breathed.

I turned slowly, raising my eyebrows.

"Do you realize what you've just done?" he demanded.

"What I should have done the first day," I spat back.

He shook his head in bafflement, but I held my ground, even as cold reality seeped in.

"Don't pretend you could have sat there in silence for five days while a group of pretentious arsehats debated the many ways in which they could hurt you or your family and not said a single stars-damned word." Though, as I spoke the words, I wondered if he could have. Maybe it was only *my* self-control that was left constantly wanting.

He shook his head, somewhere between sadness and frustration. Before he could come up with a response, Iiro appeared behind him, his features a mask of anger.

"Congratulations, Princess Rowan." His tone was acerbic. "Now that you've challenged their pride and their bravery and mocked the sacrifices of their loved ones, it's safe to say you've managed to lose what little support you had garnered."

Iiro glared at me. His words were sobering.

Tendrils of fear crept down my spine, the weight of my outburst finally sinking in. "At least they have a few days to calm down before the vote. I'll just...win them over again."

Iiro didn't dignify that with a response. He only looked meaningfully at Theo before turning back to the tent. Theo's expression turned thoughtful, but before I could question it, Lord Evander strolled out of the tent.

He examined Theo's features, then mine, before letting out a low whistle. "You know, Korhonan, I never took you for a sociopath. But the two of you seem awfully...close. Yet when the Princess manages to piss off an entire council that would just as soon let her burn as douse the fire, you don't show a trace of fear. Interesting."

He walked away before giving us a chance to respond.

It was the second time he had indicated that Iiro and Theo were keeping something from me. I would have brushed it aside, would have written it off as more of the lord's baiting, but the expression on Theo's face stopped me short.

It was guilt.

CHAPTER 49

Theo led me to an out-of-the-way clearing by the river, walking far enough that we had a relative degree of privacy. Or maybe he was smart enough to know that I needed that time to rein my temper in.

When he finally came to a stop, it was me who spoke first.

"What aren't you telling me?" My eyes didn't leave his, dissecting his features for any signs that he was hiding something.

He swallowed, looking around before he finally spoke. "There is a way to remove you from the scrutiny and the power of the Summit."

My mind reeled. "And I had to hear this from Lord Arseling because?"

"I was going to tell you—" he began before I cut him off.

"But you thought it was so much more fun to watch me squirm and dance for the Council?"

He huffed out an irritable breath. "No, I just—I didn't want you to feel forced into anything."

"Like death?" I suggested sarcastically.

"Like marriage." He practically shouted the word, and I took a step back.

"What?" My voice was a sharp contrast to his, a whisper that was quickly swallowed up by the sound of the rushing river beside us.

"I told you before, Clan wives are protected." He was calm again.

I blinked. "You want me to marry Iiro?" Would Inessa and I be sister-wives? Did they do that here?

Theo's lip curled in disgust, and he shook his head. "Storms, Rowan. No. It applies to the heirs as well."

Oh. "Oh." That was all I could seem to say, suddenly feeling very foolish for reasons I couldn't quite put my finger on.

Was this why he had brought up marriage before?

It was a way out of death, and I knew that I should grasp hold of it, but there were a hundred reasons for us not to get married. My breaths started coming faster, the trees of the clearing blurring around the edges until the crimson edged out the gold and orange and brown.

"*This* is why I didn't tell you." He sighed. "I know it isn't what you want, and I didn't think it would come up. It never occurred to me that they would actually vote against you. They wouldn't have, if you had just done what we talked about and—"

"And what, exactly? Continued to stand by silently while they threatened every member of my family? I will never be that person, Theo."

"Then you won't survive here!" His voice rose before he visibly collected himself. "You won't survive...this."·He gestured around us, defeat tugging his shoulders downward.

"Unless I'm a clan wife..." I responded quietly.

He nodded. My thoughts were a maelstrom. In a way, this would solve several issues at once. Hadn't I asked for a marriage that benefited my kingdom? An alliance with Socair would certainly satisfy that requirement.

But, that was when I assumed it would be in Lochlann, where I could see my family any time I wanted to and nothing else seemed to matter.

Doing this meant I would stay here, in Socair, cut off from my family for half of the year. Alone, except for Theo.

Theo, who held me and kissed me and defended me and *loved* me.

It was all too much to process. "Can I think about this for a day?" I asked. "I know there isn't much time left, but just until tomorrow."

He nodded, a sharp dip of his head. "Of course." But I didn't miss the edge of hurt in his tone.

I hated myself for putting it there, but this was the rest of my life on the line.

Or the lack thereof.

CHAPTER 50

I wasn't sure if I felt worse or somehow relieved when Theo, ever the gentleman, walked me over to Mila before making his excuses to be elsewhere at the dance. We had been here for nearly two hours, and he still hadn't come back yet.

Mila silently handed me another glass of medovukha as we watched the couples twirl under the stars. Everyone had given me a wide berth when I arrived, and had made a point to avoid me ever since.

I certainly didn't miss Sir Mikhail's lechery or Lord Evander's insults, even if I was surprised the latter hadn't taken his chance to gloat. He was preoccupied tonight, though, making his way around the room to converse with the dukes.

I took a long drink of the honey wine, hoping it would stir up the dredges of my black humor and help me find a way to laugh about what I had done. The first two glasses hadn't helped, but I held out hope for the third, downing the rest of the liquid in one gulp.

Nope. Still nothing.

I walked over to the refreshment table and was about to ladle more of the wine into my glass when a familiar voice sounded beside me.

"Would you care for something a little stronger?" Sir Arès proffered his flask. "Finest vodka in Socair."

"Yes, please." I said, taking the container and pouring a hefty dose of the alcohol into my glass.

He chuckled when I handed it back, much emptier than before.

"Maybe you are more Socairan than I realized," he muttered, taking a swig straight from the flask.

"Just nowhere near Socairan enough," I countered under my breath.

Arès sighed. "You really didn't do yourself any favors today," he added after taking another drink.

"I know," I admitted.

"I will speak to the other dukes, but I doubt it will change things." With a final sympathetic look, he walked away, leaving me alone once again.

I appreciated his unexpected kindness, even if his assessment of my predicament was grim. Scanning the room, my eyes snagged on Theo across the dance floor. Seeing the flicker of pain in his gaze as he looked at me nearly cracked my chest wide open.

Swallowing back the lump that had formed in my throat, I walked back over to Mila, mostly in an effort to keep myself from going to Theo. My presence abruptly cut off the conversation she was having with the lord next to her since he scurried away like I might give him leprosy.

She didn't seem to mind, though, only went back to

giving me the same hopelessly sad look that she had been shooting my way all night.

"Stop staring at me like that, Mila," I said without looking at her.

Guilt pricked at my insides, but I couldn't bring myself to tell her about the possibility of marriage.

She took a deep breath and exhaled before speaking. "When Father told me what you did, I—"

"I'm not like you, Mila," I interjected softly. "I am not Socairan, and holding my tongue when those men sat in my presence and threatened my family..." I trailed off, squeezing my eyes shut, opening them only when Mila's hand wrapped around mine.

"I don't blame you for that. I blame them for putting you in this position." She glared at Lord Evander and Sir Nils, who had their heads together in a whispered conversation. "There has to be something we can do. This can't be it."

A swell of gratitude rose up in me. In the handful of days we had known one another, Mila had been a truer friend than anyone outside of my family had back home.

"It's not over yet," I reminded her. It was as close as I could come to telling her there was hope, yet.

She squeezed my hand, and we passed the rest of the time in silence..

With Mila and Theo, maybe things wouldn't be so terrible in Socair. I wouldn't have my family, but two friends were far better than none.

The pressure in my chest eased slightly as I considered it. Maybe Theo was right. Maybe I was being ridiculous.

It certainly wasn't like I could trust my own judgment these days.

We didn't go to the sauna that night. Instead, we went straight back to the Elk tent and freshened up with bowls of river water and a clean cloth.

Inessa helped me to change, and I took longer than I needed to cleaning up. Everyone was in their bedrolls by the time I crawled into mine.

The air in the small room was thick with tension, an invisible line cleaving the space between Theo and me.

His chest rose and fell unevenly, barely visible in the low light of the lantern. If it weren't for that, I wouldn't have known he was awake. Minutes ticked by, and the quiet stretched on until even our breathing felt intrusive and overly loud.

Finally, I couldn't take it anymore. I couldn't stand the fact that I had hurt him, especially when he was willing to make this sacrifice for me.

"You know that I care about you." The silence shattered like a crystal vase on a bare stone floor.

His breathing hitched, the only indication he was listening to me.

"But is this really how you want to choose your bride?" I questioned.

Another moment went by before he turned over to face me.

"I always knew Iiro would arrange my marriage, and I seem to recall you telling me that you asked your mother to arrange yours. So it would appear that you don't care who you marry, so long as it isn't me."

I opened my mouth to argue, but in a way, he wasn't wrong. He was the only person I had actual feelings for, and I wanted no part of that. I thought about what he had said, that loving someone was a ridiculous reason not to marry them, and I forced myself to give him a better truth.

"It isn't that I don't want to marry you. What scares me is that I do, but come on, Theo. Don't pretend this would be easy for either of us. Your people hate me, and half of them think I'm cursed."

"Not you," he argued. "Just...your hair."

"That isn't better, unless you want me to shave my head for the rest of my life."

He reached a hand out to my hair, twirling a strand between his fingers. "Please don't. I happen to like your cursed hair."

Amusement colored his tone, but I huffed out an irritable breath. "I'm serious, Theo. What happens when our children come out with *cursed* red hair? Have you thought about that? It's a very dominant trait! All of my siblings, all of my cousins on my mother's side, we all have very bright, very red hair."

He laughed outright then. At least one of us was in better spirits. "Storms, Rowan, the things you say."

"I'm not wrong." I jutted out my chin.

"No, you're not wrong. But our people are not entirely unreasonable. They would come around, once they saw that you weren't so different from us." He leaned forward, pressing his lips against my forehead.

"But who knows how long that would take," I pressed.

"And that's just one thing. I'm only saying, there are so many things to think about and figure out, things we would have time to discuss if we waited."

"I understand that, Rowan." Exasperation laced his tone. "And in a perfect world, we would, but you're pitting working through a few issues against the fact that you might *die* in three days."

I let out a slow whoosh of air. "There is that."

Silence yawned between us once again, but this time it was filled with slightly less tension.

"Well, I suppose we can see how much actual damage was done tomorrow," I finally said.

Not that the way the dukes had acted at the dance left much room for hope.

Regardless, Theo seemed somewhat mollified by that. He nodded his agreement, then rolled back over and was snoring softly within minutes.

But I stayed awake, watching the shadow of firelight flicker on the fabric of the tent while my thoughts chased themselves in an unrelenting loop.

And still, I was not prepared when morning came.

CHAPTER 51

The strain in the room with Theo last night was nothing compared to what awaited me in the Summit tent.

No one argued. No one even respectfully debated.

No one spoke at all.

Not Mikhail, whose face was smug, or Nils from Wolf, who was grimly satisfied. Evander drummed his fingers in a bored pattern, but didn't open his mouth.

Even Sir Arès, who looked at me with sympathy, kept his lips clamped firmly shut. It was their silent protest. Their way of showing me that they would sit here until the eighth day as they were honor-bound to do, but their decision had been made.

Dread pooled in my stomach, but I kept my features in a semblance of calm neutrality. There was nothing I could do or say to change their minds now.

Even Iiro must have known, because he didn't try to speak or sway them. I couldn't entirely blame him for not

281

wanting to throw his lot in with mine now that I knew how important these alliances were.

An hour stretched into two, then three.

I reflected again on the unforgiving Socairan mentality, the way they seemed to believe the punishment for everything was death. Smuggling. Disobedience. A single outburst.

It was hard to believe this had all started with a few bottles of vodka. And now I was here, walking a tenuous tightrope between marriage and death.

There really was only one thing to do.

I turned to Theo, forcing a bit of lightheartedness into my features.

This was a good thing. For all the stupid things I had done, I would finally make a good decision. Marriage into Socair would help build a bridge between our kingdoms. There could be peace.

And Theo would make an amazing husband, protective and kind and gorgeous. We could get through life in Socair, together. Whatever their other faults, obviously Clan Bear had gotten over their Lochlann Clan Wife.

Elk would, too, in time.

More than all of that, I loved Theo. And he loved me. The fact was that the damage was done. Walking away from him now would kill me just as much as if something happened down the line. It was too late to turn back, so it was time to go all in.

With that thought, my smile came more genuinely. When he caught my gaze and subtle nod, he crept over to crouch next to me.

I leaned over and whispered as quietly as I could. "I accept, on one condition."

"Oh?" He quirked an eyebrow, wariness battling happiness in his expression.

"That I never have to eat borscht again."

The corner of his lips tilted up in a wry smile. "I think that can be arranged."

Then he broke out into a smile in truth, one that made my heart feel lighter in my chest. It was hard to remember why I had hesitated on this before when it seemed so simple now.

Theo shot Iiro a meaningful look, and Iiro's shoulders sagged in what might have been relief. I was a little surprised he cared so much, though maybe that was more about saving face.

Iiro got to his feet. The dukes murmured a bit, looking at him with furrowed brows. Evander sat up straighter in his seat, suspicion and what might have been panic edging out the indifference in his features.

A lifetime seemed to pass before Iiro cleared his throat to speak. A hush fell once more, the room thrumming with the anticipation of his next words.

But the voice that rang out did not belong to Iiro.

It belonged to Evander, who was hastily getting to his feet as he spoke in a deceptively bland tone. "I claim my family's blood debt against the Pendragon family."

CHAPTER 52

The words seemed to echo in the unnatural hush that had fallen over the tent, while I racked my brain for everything Theo had told me about blood debts.

There wasn't much, though. Only that they were enforceable across clans. I had focused so much on the Clan Wife thing, I hadn't given it much thought. But surely I would have had to kill someone? I hadn't done anything to stupid blasted Evander or his clan.

"On what grounds?" Arès asked what I wanted to know.

Evander's gaze flicked over me, his features tightening with disdain.

"Her parents facilitated and witnessed the wedding that broke the agreement with my father, which led to the war." He looked around at the clan leaders, meeting each of their eyes.

"I wasn't even born then!" I protested.

"It doesn't matter," Evander shrugged. "It's your family's debt against mine, and it is within my rights to pursue that."

"A broken agreement does not constitute a blood debt,' Iiro hissed.

"No, but the resulting war does. More specifically, the murder of my father's brother that King Logan committed when he blew up the tunnels." He looked pointedly at the men of the council, his tone dripping with condescension. "Remind me, does *that* constitute a blood debt?"

"It does," Mikhail helpfully chimed in. *Bastard.*

I had so many questions about what was going on that I couldn't seem to voice a single one.

"Regardless," Iiro cut in again. "Before I was interrupted by a boy who shouldn't have a voice in this council at all, I was preparing to announce my brother's betrothal to the princess."

Theo got to his feet, standing behind me and placing his hands on my shoulders in a clear message.

"Remind me," Iiro said sarcastically to Evander. "Are clan wives subject to blood debts?"

"Of course not." Evander didn't miss a beat. "But a betrothed does not a wife make."

"Then they will wed tonight," Iiro supplied.

I leaned back into Theo, trying to take comfort in his steady presence, but his body was thrumming with fury or panic.

"You cannot enforce the protection of a clan wife *after* I claim my blood debt. That would make a mockery of our most sacred laws." Evander looked to the other dukes for support.

I studied their features, looking for a single reason to

hope that there might be a way out of this—whatever *this* was—but that hope died when I saw the resignation on Arès' face.

"Lord Evander is correct," he said reluctantly. "If we allow marriage as an avenue of escape from a blood debt after the claim is staked, the law would be all but useless."

I finally found my voice. "Is someone going to tell me what this blood debt even means?" *Am I going to die, after all?*

"It doesn't matter," Theo growled, "because he isn't taking you."

Evander responded as though Theo hadn't spoken. "It means your life belongs to my clan for the one that was stolen from us."

"So you're going to kill me because my mother helped her best friend avoid a marriage to a *barbarian,* and my father defended his kingdom from a war your people started?"

Evander's eyes narrowed at my insult, but he shook his head. "No, I don't think I'll kill you yet. I think you'll make a very entertaining pet."

Theo lunged forward, his sword already in his hand, and blind panic overtook me. The punishment for shedding blood at the Summit was, hadn't he said it was death? Or was it worse than death?

Either way, I couldn't let that happen to Theo. Not because of the abhorrent lord from Clan Bear, and certainly not because of me.

"No!" I shouted, moving to stand between them. "Don't. I'll go."

I met Theo's incredulous stare with pleading in my own.

"Stand down, Theodore," Iiro ordered in a harsh voice. "You know what I will have to do if you spill blood here."

Theo looked more furious than I had ever seen him, his hazel eyes practically glowing with ire. His jaw worked, and he shook his head furiously, no words coming.

"Very well," Arès said, his calm tone at odds with the regret in his features. "It is decided. Lord Evander will claim his rightful blood debt. Princess Rowan is now the lawful property of Clan Bear. Any preexisting arrangements, including...betrothals, are henceforth terminated. She will return with Evander to his lands, where she will live out the remainder of her life, and..." He looked pointedly at Evander then. "And Bear alone will deal with whatever consequences the Lochlann brings upon them."

My heart stopped beating in my chest as the reality of my situation hit home.

The rest of my life as Evander's...slave? Plaything?

Suddenly, the Summit's many creative ideas for my death weren't sounding quite so bad.

CHAPTER 53

Numbness stole over me.

I'm never going home.

I'm never going to see my family again.

Evander's voice broke into my thoughts. "Come along, my little Lemmikki."

I turned my head mutely to Theo for a translation, and his hands clenched into fists. "It means pet," he spat out.

Pet.

Pet?

His *pet?*

Absolutely the stars-damned-hell not.

Anger broke through my disbelief, and I glared at Evander. "I am not your anything, least of all your pet. And I will come *after* I've said my goodbyes. It's the least you can do."

He raised his eyebrows in mock offense, though there was a bitter edge to his expression. "The least I can do? After I already rescued you from your reluctant nuptials. I believe I'll add ungrateful to your lengthy list of flaws."

My lips parted in fury. *Eavesdropping bastard.* Before I could form a response, he spoke again.

"Very well. Fifteen minutes, but stay where I can see you." His mouth formed a cruel smile. "Never let it be said that I am not...accommodating."

His use of that word felt intentional, like all of his words, a sharply honed dagger thrown with precise, unfailing aim. My heart beat a furious rhythm within my chest, and my vision was swimming. This was all happening too fast.

Clamping my hand around Theo's wrist, I dragged him away before he could change his mind and go after Evander after all. It would have been tempting, were it not for the consequences if Theo won.

And the fact that, after seeing them spar, I wasn't entirely sure that he would.

When we were out of earshot, though still under Evander's spiteful gaze, I finally stopped. Theo turned, cupping my face in his warm hands.

It was an effort not to lean into his touch and let him comfort me. All of that was about to be ripped away, though, and I needed to brace myself.

"I won't say goodbye to you. This isn't over," he said. "I will find a way to get you out of this. And when the mountain pass opens, I will send word to your father."

My heart dropped into my stomach. Da' would never let this stand. *Ever.* After everything, there would still be a war because of me.

But it wasn't like I could stop him from finding out, either.

"Promise me, you'll take care of Davin, and get him

home safely. Our family can't handle losing us both." My voice broke on that last word.

All the times I had worried what the Summit would decide, it had felt far away and not quite real. Now, Evander had come along with an entirely different fate, and it might be worse than death.

"They are not losing you, and neither am I. We will find a way, I promise." Theo's arms came around me, his lips crushing against mine.

After everything I told myself before, I caved and allowed myself a single moment to sink into him, to accept the comfort of his words and his warmth and the promises we both knew he couldn't keep.

Then I abruptly backed away, blinking away the tears that had formed in my eyes.

"Tell my family—" I stopped. There were so many things I wanted to say to them, but nothing that felt like nearly enough. "Just tell them that I love them. And that I'm sorry. For all of this."

If I stayed with him another moment, I would break down, and I'd be damned if I let Evander see me that way. With one final squeeze of Theo's hand, I moved to leave.

CHAPTER 54

E vander wrapped a hand around my arm and led me toward his carriage, which had appeared on the small road near the tent during the time I was *not* saying goodbye to Theo.

He certainly wasn't wasting any time in claiming his debt and leaving the Summit. My pulse pounded in my ears, but I was desperate not to give him a reaction. He would enjoy that too much.

Two more guards appeared, carrying the trunks that Mila had given me, loading them onto the carriage. They wore matching black livery with a white outline of a bear stitched onto the upper right arm, identical to the one on Evander's long coat.

Inessa followed just behind them, her face pinched with worry until her eyes met mine. Whatever she saw in them changed her expression to grief.

In an uncharacteristic display of emotion, she moved toward me. Evander dropped his hand, stepping back, and Inessa enveloped me in her embrace. She didn't say anything for the several seconds she held me, nor when she moved away to stand next to her husband.

Iiro only gave me a grim nod, his features tight as he looked between his brother's despairing face and mine. I returned his nod, forcibly wrenching my gaze from where Theo was openly glaring at Evander.

Turning back toward the carriage, I took a deep breath as one of the guards opened the door, waiting for me to enter. My legs didn't want to carry me forward, my chest rising and falling in time with my rapid breaths.

But there was no part of me that would let Evander drag me away kicking and screaming.

I had just taken a single, tiny step forward when a panicked voice shouted my name from down the road.

Mila's eyes were red and she was running toward me, calling for me to wait.

Evander groaned behind me, and I narrowly resisted the urge to grab Theo's sword and stab him myself. Only the fact that it was a fight I couldn't win stayed my temper.

Mila crashed into me, wrapping me in a fierce hug that nearly knocked me to the ground.

"No. He can't do this." Her raspy voice broke. "You can't do this!" She yelled at Evander who stood there silently.

"Mila." I pulled away from her, looking up into her tear-strewn face. "It's all right," I lied.

She wrapped her arms around me again and leaned down to whisper in my ear.

"I will come to you as soon as I can. Just..." She took a breath. "Stay safe until then. Please."

I nodded wordlessly. What could I really say to that?

Mila finally pulled herself away, and the only face left in my line of vision was Theo's.

My breathing hitched as I watched the turmoil in his eyes. I didn't say goodbye, and true to his word, neither did he. He just watched with a pained expression as I turned to Evander.

My new *owner*.

Evander gestured toward the carriage door and I clambered in without another word. He climbed into the seat next to me, his expression as cold as everything else about him.

A footman closed the door behind him, shutting us inside the carriage. It was enormous, but I couldn't shake the feeling of being sealed inside a tomb.

Because there was no escaping this.

I belonged to Evander to do with as he wished.

My fists clenched around my skirts, and my heart galloped within my chest. Somehow, I had found myself in a far worse situation than the one before, headed toward a future that whispered promises of pain and death.

All for a couple of bottles of stars-damned vodka.

Pronunciation Guide

Rowan	ROE-an (long O)
Davin	DAV-in (short A)
Theo	THEE-oe
Iiro	EER-oe
Avani	ah-VAHN-ee
Mila	MEE-lah
Venla	VEN-lah
Inessa	in-ES-ah
Evander	ee-VAN-der
Socair	soe-CARE
Lochlann	LOCK-lan
Chridhe	CREE
Hagail	ha-GALE
Borscht	borsht
Lemmikki	lem-EEK-ee

Clan Elk
Duke: Iiro
Colors: Navy & Tan

Clan Bison
Duke: Ivan
Colors: Orange & Gray

Clan Ram
Duke: Mikhail
Colors: White & Red

Clan Viper
Duke: Andreyev
Colors: Green & Gold

Clan Wolf
Duke: Nils
Colors: Gray & White

Clan Lynx
Duke: Arès
Colors: Teal & Gold

Clan Crane
Duke: Danil
Colors: Yellow & Black

Clan Eagle
Duke: Timofey
Colors: White & Brown

Clan Bear
Duke: Aleksander
Colors: Black & White

A MESSAGE FROM US

We need your help!

Did you know that authors, in particular indie authors like us, make their living on reviews? If you liked this book, or even if you didn't, please take a moment to let people know on all of the major review platforms like; Amazon, Goodreads, and/or Bookbub!

(Social Media gushing is also highly encouraged!)

Remember, reviews don't have to be long. It can be as simple as whatever star rating you feel comfortable with and an: 'I loved it!' or: 'Not my cup of tea...'

Now that that's out of the way, if you want to come shenanigate with us, rant and rave about these books and others, get access to awesome giveaways, exclusive content and some pretty ridiculous live videos, come join us on Facebook at our group; Drifters and Wanderers

ROBIN'S
ACKNOWLEDGMENTS

My first thank you, as always, is to my bestie/co-author for staying up for days on end in a hotel room with a barking dog next to us and the world's smelliest cauliflower just to get this done on time. We did it!

And thank you for going along with my crazy hair-brained idea to throw our lineup out the window in favor of Rowan's story, for agreeing to write the middle sister first, and for generally putting up with me through seventy-five thousand renditions of "this plot doesn't feel right yet."

Your gorgeous maps and perfectly culled playlists and creative clan flags brought every aspect of this world to life even before you put a single word to the page.

Mostly, thank you for shaping Rowan into this hilarious, weather-toe-having, loins-girding, ridiculousness that she is. Because of you, diving back into Lochlann has been everything I dreamed it would be, and I wish we never had to leave.

To our Alpha/Beta/Awesome Team, I seriously couldn't be more grateful for you guys! I can't imagine another team being as flexible with these deadlines or rereading as many times as y'all did, and if that wasn't awesome enough, your group chat gave us life. <3

To our ARC readers, our readers, and all you Bookstagrammers out spreading the word and making us glorious images, we couldn't do any of this without you and we wouldn't want to!

Amanda, you helped us beat this cover into submission and planned TWO amazing tours for us in the process. Thank you so much for your patience and your help and your humor, but most of all for your friendship. Also...(-)(-)

To the awesomest of Jamies, thank you so much for once again editing on a deadline. I'm sorry we couldn't give you more Davin to make up for it, but I promise, that's coming! Can you believe you've stuck with me for THIRTEEN books, not even counting all the smaller projects? Every book, I'm surprised all over again that you haven't fired me yet. :P

Finally, to my husband. Thank you for your never-ending well of patience when I work long hours and rant on end about a plot hole or gush nonstop about a fictitious romance. Thank you for taking care of our babies and staying up late so we can spend time together after my workday ends. I could never do any of this without your love and support.

And a special thank you to my babies, for giving me so many reasons to laugh, for showing me a different way to look at the world, and putting me in the happy headspace to write books like these.

ELLE'S ACKNOWLEDGMENTS

How do I even begin to account for this journey back into Lochlann?

Robin, thank you as always for being the best friend and co-author I could dream of. This book was like going home in so many ways and was the breath of fresh air that we needed.

I've missed our Lochlann shenanigans and this world and these characters so very much and I will forever be grateful for that day you called me to say "Let's push everything else to the side and do a next generation story..."

I can't wait to continue Rowan's journey and all of the rest of our Lochlann stories with you!! (But please... no more cauliflower on writing weekends... Or barking dogs... Or serial-killer style hotels in Denver with no working phones... Maybe let's just hit the beach instead?)

Next, I want to give a HUGE thank you to our amazing ALPHA and BETA team... You girls are seriously the best and we could not have done this without you! Lissa, Emily, Rachel, Michelle, Ali, Sarah, Hope & Erin - Thank you, thank you, thank you for your late night reads and rereads and all of your hilarious commentary and input!

A special shoutout to Sarah for teaching us the German word for a very punchable face... That is a gift that will keep on giving...

Jamie Peanut-Butter Whiskey Holmes- You are the best editor we could have and we are still constantly in awe that you continue to put up with us project after project! Thank you for always believing in us, even when we didn't believe in ourselves. We love you to the moon and back!

To our Drifters and Wanderers, MoonTree Readers, ARC readers and Social Media supporters - Thank you for being so amazing and supportive and for being so excited to dive back into Lochlann with us!

Amanda Steele - You beautiful soul you! Thank you for your constant support, feedback on covers, titles and general authorish things. You have been in our corner from day one, and we LOVE you and your amazing company Book of Matches Media!

To our phenomenal author friends, Sophie Davis, Jesikah Sundin, Alisha Klapheke, Melanie Karsak, Heather Renee, Lichelle Slater, Candace Robinson, Eliza Tilton, and so so many more. Thank you for constantly checking in our sanity and progress, for being such amazing team players and the best author friends that we could have! Your late night messages and chats were vital to our survival this summer with all of these projects. <3

And finally, to my husband... Thank you for putting up with our insane deadlines this summer, and really, for the past three years all so I could pursue this dream I didn't know I had. You are the peanut-butter to my Oreos, the Bailey's to my coffee and the best friend I could have. Thank you for holding down the fort, dealing with my panic attacks, listening to me rant and rave about a new or unyielding storyline, and mostly for taking care of our two beautiful boys while I hid away in my writing cave.

I love you more than all the words in all the books in all the world.

ABOUT THE AUTHORS

Elle and Robin can usually be found on road trips around the US haunting taco-festivals and taking selfies with unsuspecting Spice Girls impersonators.

They have a combined PH.D in Faery Folklore and keep a romance advice column under a British pen-name for raccoons. They have a rare blood type made up solely of red wine and can only write books while under the influence of the full moon.

Between the two of them they've created a small army of insatiable humans and when not wrangling them into their cages, they can be seen dancing jigs and sacrificing brownie batter to the pits of their stomachs.

And somewhere between their busy schedules, they still find time to create words and put them into books.

ALSO BY ELLE & ROBIN

The Lochlann Treaty Series:

Winter's Captive

Spring's Rising

Summer's Rebellion

Autumn's Reign

Twisted Pages Series:

Of Thorns and Beauty

Of Beasts and Vengeance

Of Glass and Ashes

Of Thieves and Shadows

Coming May 2023:

Of Songs and Silence

The World Apart Series By Robin D. Mahle:

The Fractured Empire

The Tempest Sea

The Forgotten World

The Ever Falls

Unfabled Series:

Promises and Pixie Dust

Made in United States
Troutdale, OR
04/02/2024

18879256R00195